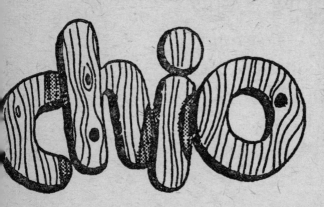

Based on Walt Disney Productions' full length
cartoon feature film

This adaptation by

DERRY MOFFATT

NEW ENGLISH LIBRARY
TIMES MIRROR

Other stories from Disney cartoon feature films
and available in the NEL series

DUMBO

LADY AND THE TRAMP

SNOW WHITE AND THE SEVEN DWARFS

SONG OF THE SOUTH

ROBIN HOOD

SLEEPING BEAUTY

FIRST NEL PAPERBACK EDITION SEPTEMBER 1975

NEL Books are published by
New English Library Limited from Barnard's Inn,
Holborn, London EC1.
Made and printed in Great Britain by
Hunt Barnard Printing Ltd, Aylesbury, Bucks.
Typesetting by The Yale Press Ltd, London SE25

45002690 6

INTRODUCTION

When you wish upon a star
Makes no difference who you are,
Anything your heart desires
Will come to you.
If your heart is in your dreams
No request is too extreme,
When you wish upon a star,
As dreamers do.
Fate is kind—she brings to
those who love,
The sweet fulfilment of their secret longing.
Like a bolt out of the blue
Fate steps in and sees you through,
When you wish upon a star
Your dreams come true.

Isn't that a beautiful song? It is my
favourite. My name is Jiminy Cricket and even
if I say so myself I'm a very special kind of
cricket.

In a way I'm quite a little showman. Like
right now as I sit on a shelf in the spotlight.
Hey, where is the spot? Somebody is always
trying to spoil my act. Look where the spotlight
is now — focused on a beautiful book. Well,
I'll just take my umbrella and hat and sit on
top of the volume.

There, that's better. Now — where was I?
Oh, yes — the song . . .

Wasn't it pretty, huh? I'll bet a lot of folks

don't believe that about a wish coming true — do you? Well, I didn't either. Of course, I'm just a cricket singing my way from hearth to hearth, but let me tell you what made me change my mind.

Excuse me while I slide down the book. Isn't it handsome? Genuine leather binding, too. And just look at that lettering: P-I-N-O-C-C-H-I-O. That is a name which rolls off the tongue. Now to open the gold clasp and see what is written inside.

One night, a long time ago — oh gosh, the pages are falling back on me. Wait until I fix them! A candle-holder should do the trick. I'll pull it over with the crook of my umbrella. There — that's got it!

I say, what wonderful pictures inside. Makes you want to travel, eh? Like I did . . . but wait, I'm getting ahead of myself. Let's begin again.

One night, a long time ago, my travels took me to a quaint little village. It was a beautiful night and the stars were shining like diamonds high above the rooftops of that sleepy old place. It was as pretty as a picture with the soft velvet sky hanging above the spires. In the distance the moonlit mountains formed an eerie snow-capped horizon. As I wandered along the crooked streets with their cobble-stones and flagged pavements, there wasn't a soul to be seen. The only sign of life came from the lighted window of a wood-carver's shop.

This was—uh—Geppetto's place, so I hopped over to it, carrying my carpet-bag, and peered through the window. A cheery fire glowed in the grate and it seemed a shame for its warmth to go to waste. Immediately, I decided to take up lodgings for the night. But how to get inside? Well, where there's a will there's always a way, so I crawled underneath the door dragging my carpet-bag after me.

I looked around appreciating the charm of the wood-carver's fascinating work-room. Of course, being in a strange place I wasn't taking any chances. I ran behind a table leg and peeped. I didn't know what to expect—a cricket can't be too careful, you know!

As soon as I saw there was no one about, I made myself at home. Brushing myself off I cocked my hat and strutted towards the fire. Warming my hands I got an idea and used my umbrella to draw a hot coal forward.

As I stood there warming myself, I took a good look around. You've never seen such a place. The most fantastic clocks you've ever laid eyes on, and all carved out of wood. Cute little music-boxes, each one a work of art. Shelf after shelf of toys and . . .

Leaving my lovely hot coal I hopped across the room. Something had caught my eye — a puppet. You know what I mean. One of those marionette things — all strings and joints. I had to get closer so I jumped on a chair and leapt to the work-bench.

What a cute little fellow the puppet was. I pulled one of the strings, climbed it until I was able to swing onto his nose. The tap-tap of my umbrella on its head sounded solid. A good piece of wood, too.

This was fun and I was about to enjoy myself when I heard *them*. You can imagine how I felt. A cricket isn't a very big chap and needs to be extra cautious when others are about. Which is why I'm fading from this introduction and letting the story continue just like it happened that long time ago . . .

CHAPTER ONE

Geppetto, the kindly old toy-maker, walked down the stairs to his workshop. Ahead of him gambolled Figaro, the cat with glossy black fur ornamented by a white face and four white socks which always had a freshly laundered look. A delighted smile lit the toy-maker's tired face as he approached his latest puppet, a paint-pot in his hand.

Jiminy Cricket, seated on the puppet's nose, looked up in alarm at the approaching footsteps. Swiftly grabbing the puppet strings he swung over to a shelf, then peered down. Crossing to the bench, Geppetto picked up his latest creation. 'Just a little more paint — and he's all finished! I think he'll be all right, don't you, Figaro?'

Figaro, lithe and graceful as a miniature panther, jumped onto the bench, contemplated the puppet through half-closed eyes then shrugged his shoulders. To him, it was just another puppet. The little cat watched with lively interest as Geppetto painted eyebrows on the wooden doll's face. Apart from Jiminy, hidden on the shelf, and Figaro the cat, there was also another inquisitive spectator — Cleo, the goldfish. With a flick of her fan-like tail she rose to the surface of the water, blew a few bubbles, then peered again as with a few deft touches, Geppetto skilfully brought the boy puppet's features to life.

Jiminy Cricket sat quietly gazing at the comfortable, homely scene. The coal fire in the grate burned brightly, sending streaks of blue hissing flame up the chimney. The combination of toys, clocks, puppets, warmth and love radiated an atmosphere of enchantment. Jiminy was well pleased with the lodgings he had selected for the night.

A very chirpy, intelligent cricket, he also took a pride in his appearance. He wore beige-coloured trousers, neat spats, a black coat and a red vest. On his head, balanced at a rakish angle, was a top hat. Close beside him lay his umbrella. Jiminy Cricket seldom went anywhere without his umbrella; he found it useful for a variety of purposes.

Geppetto glanced up from his labour of love and Jiminy, not wanting to be noticed, ran behind a little red wagon with blue wheels. Reaching for his umbrella he opened it out and parachuted to another shelf and hid behind a music-box. Geppetto hummed softly as he worked while Figaro dashed round and round the paint-pot slapping at the brush with his tail. From his vantage point, Jiminy grinned at the little cat's antics, admiring the way in which he delicately picked his way along the surface of the bench.

Geppetto painted a smiling mouth on his puppet and held it up. 'See! That makes a big difference,' he said warmly to Figaro.

The cat smiled, nodding his head in agreement. Cleo beamed, too. The cricket also approved of Geppetto's handiwork and said softly to himself, 'Very good . . . very, very good . . .'

At last, Geppetto laid down his brush. His puppet was completely finished. 'Now,' he said to the boy doll, 'I have just the name for you: Pinocchio!' He turned to Figaro who was washing his snowy feet. 'Do you like it, Figaro?' Figaro paused, holding a damp paw in

the air. He made a wry face and emphatically shook his head.

Geppetto looked disappointed. 'No?' he said. 'You do, don't you, Cleo?' But the goldfish didn't like the toy-maker's choice, either. Geppetto pointed. 'Well, we will leave it to little wooden-head!' Picking up the puppet he manoeuvered its strings. 'You like the name?' he asked. He manipulated the puppet to say "yes". Pleased, Geppetto released the strings. 'Ha, ha . . . that settles it.' Slapping his thigh in satisfaction he said, 'Pinocchio it is!' The little boy puppet had been christened.

Picking up Pinocchio, Geppetto walked over to the music-box. Jiminy dived out of sight beneath the instrument. Geppetto wound a key in the box, and instantly, the musicians on top of the box started to play. For Jiminy, crouching below the box, this was a calamity. The vibrations pummelled him. 'Hey! Ouch, ouch,' he yelled. 'Hey, hey . . . take it easy there! Break it up, will you?' Gingerly he crawled out from his hiding place and the revolving key knocked his hat flying. 'Whew!' Jiminy bent down and slapped his hat back on. 'Lotta downbeats in there!' he remarked, mopping his forehead, and sought refuge behind a carving.

The toy-maker was delighted with his puppet. Dancing a few steps he pulled Pinocchio's strings so that the little figure danced and jiggled. As they moved across the floor together, Figaro followed at a distance, then bounded playfully forward. Geppetto started to sing:

Little wooden-head go play your part,
Bring a little joy to every heart,
Little do you know
And yet it's true,
That I'm mighty proud of you.
Little wooden feet, and best of all,
Little wooden seat in case you . . .

He broke off singing to lift Pinocchio high in the air, then bring him down to the ground beside Figaro. The little cat leapt swiftly out of the way and Geppetto laughed. 'In case you fall,' he sang, finishing the last line of his song. Figaro scowled, raising his paw in the air, ready to take a swipe at Pinocchio. Geppetto petted him before turning his attentions back to his newest creation. 'Aw, how graceful, my little wooden-head,' he said with an air of satisfaction.

With the toy-maker's help, Pinocchio continued to dance and pivot in the most extraordinary and life-like way, coming closer and closer to Cleo. The pretty goldfish shied away, exhaling bubbles. She was not at all sure about the latest addition to their household.

'Cleo,' said Geppetto manipulating Pinocchio onto the bench, '...meet Pinocchio!' Pinocchio peered over the edge of the bowl and raised his hat. 'Say how do you do,' prompted the toy-maker to his goldfish. Obligingly, Cleo blinked her eyes, swished her tail, flirting with the wooden boy. She was a sweet-natured, responsive creature, always eager to please.

Figaro was fully absorbed in washing his face. When Geppetto brought the puppet within close range he hastily backed away. 'Say hello to Figaro!' Pinocchio reached over and patted the cat, cuddling up to him.

Then Geppetto picked up the puppet. 'Up we go ... ah, you're a cute little fellow ... and that smile! You know, I ...' Figaro rushed over to Geppetto, meouwing loudly and rubbing against his leg. Geppetto's sock fell down and as he bent to pull it up he said, 'Figaro, you rascal ... jealous, huh!' He scooped the cat into his arms and turning to his marionette, said, 'You know, Pinocchio, I think Figaro's jealous of you.' Undoubtedly, Figaro was. With lightning fury he slapped Pinocchio with his snowy paw.

Geppetto stroked Figaro's silky head. 'Ho, don't worry, Figaro, I still . . .' One of the numerous clocks on the wall struck the hour . . . then another . . . and another. 'Oh, oh!' murmured Geppetto, placing both puppet and cat on to a bench. All the clocks continued to strike one after another; the bee clock, the duck puddle clock, then the mama and the baby cuckoo clocks. Each had their own individual sound and the noise was deafening. Geppetto, one eyebrow raised, withdrew his watch from his pocket, examining it critically. 'I wonder what the time is,' he muttered. 'Ah, it's nine o'clock.' He reached for Figaro, picking him up gently.

'It's getting late . . . come on now, we'll go to bed.' He yawned, gently tweaking Pinocchio's nose. 'Goodnight Pinocchio, little funny face.' Slowly he moved away from the bench, reluctant to leave his new puppet. 'Goodnight, Cleo . . . my little water-baby.' Cleo, looking very pleased, turned over on her back and Geppetto, chuckling, tickled her tummy. Figaro, who had jumped from the toy-maker's arms to peer into the fish bowl, prepared to jump off the table.

'Figaro,' rebuked Geppetto, 'you say good-night, too!' Figaro scowled; he was still in a bad humour, Cleo sidled to the edge and kissed the glass with her puckered mouth. Obstinate, Figaro sat with his shoulders hunched, but beneath Geppetto's penetrating gaze he was forced to give the bowl a quick lick before turning away. It wasn't much of a gesture, but it was better than no gesture at all. Cleo spun rapidly round in the water and blinked shyly in Figaro's direction.

Geppetto smiled and picking up Figaro again he whispered to Cleo, 'Now, go to sleep, my little mermaid. Goodnight!' Cleo had a castle in her bowl and she swum over to it and settled inside. Resting her golden face on a fin, she was soon fast asleep, blowing clouds of tiny bubbles.

Jiminy Cricket was still on the shelf. Everyone was going to bed so he removed his coat, rolling it into a pillow. Stifling a huge yawn he muttered, 'Ho hum . . . this is my idea of comfort.' He removed his top hat, then settled himself on top of a violin. After another yawn, he kicked off his patent shoes, closed his eyes and wiggled his toes. 'Solid comfort . . . ahh!' he said blissfully.

Geppetto undressed, pulling a long nightshirt over his head, then climbed into an elaborately carved bed which he had made himself. After lighting the candle on the bedside table he stuffed tobacco into his pipe and leaned back contentedly, puffing smoke into the air. Figaro hadn't wasted any time . . . already he was curled comfortably on the quilt, a shiny black and white ball of fur, purring gently. Geppetto looked at his pet with affection. Then his eyes strayed towards Pinocchio. In the faint, flickering light of the candle he could see the little puppet's bright, smiling features. They filled his heart with a strange longing. 'Huh! Just look at him, Figaro,' he mused. 'He almost looks alive.' The little cat opened one sleepy eye and rolled over, yawning. He wished that Geppetto would settle down and sleep, too. 'Wouldn't it be nice,' went on Geppetto suppressing a sigh, 'if he was a *real* boy!' Sadly, he blinked. 'Oh well, come on, we go to sleep!' Thoughtfully, he hung up his pipe and snuffed out the candle. Snuggling low in the comfortable bed, he pulled the covers about his ears. Figaro sighed contentedly and re-settled himself, a smile on his snowy face. At last! But no . . . the tranquility wasn't to last.

'Aw, Figaro . . .' Geppetto sat up in bed. 'I forgot to open the window.'

Figaro scowled in utter disgust, kicked the covers from his feet and instead of leaping from the bed which was his intention, managed to fall out on his face. Disgruntled, he picked himself up, padding across the room. Climbing onto the ledge he kicked the window furiously to open it and nearly fell out. He grimaced . . . it really wasn't his night!

The open window had revealed a beautiful, starlit night. 'Oh Figaro — look!' Geppetto sat up in bed pointing his finger and speaking excitedly. The little cat raised his ears as he sat perched on the windowsill. 'Look,' continued Geppetto. 'The wishing star!'

Jiminy Cricket, cosily curled up on the violin, overheard the toy-maker's comments. Turning over, he managed to peer up at the twinkling wishing star.

Geppetto climbed from his bed and kneeled down at the window. Longingly, he looked into the night and clasping his hands together, said:

Star light, star bright,
First star I see tonight,
I wish I may, I wish I might
Have the wish I make tonight!

Daintily, Figaro raised his paw to his mouth to cover a yawn. 'Figaro, do you know what I wished?' Figaro shook his head from side to side wishing that he was back in bed. Just to humour Geppetto he grinned and waited. 'I wished that my little Pinocchio might be a *real* boy!'

Geppetto rose from his knees and walked slowly back to bed. 'Wouldn't that be nice?' he murmured as Figaro jumped onto the quilt, '. . . a *real* boy!'

Jiminy from his perch on the violin nodded his head. 'A very lovely thought, but not at all practical.'

Figaro purred loudly as Geppetto scratched his back, closing his eyes in ecstasy. 'A *real* boy!' repeated Geppetto. Gradually, the sleepy toy-maker sank lower and lower in his comfortable bed until his hand dropped off Figaro's back; soon he was snoring. Figaro, after opening one eye, delicately picked his way up to the pillow, then burrowed beneath the covers, snuggling close. Soon, their combined snores mingled with the loud ticking of the clocks!

CHAPTER TWO

Jiminy Cricket wanted to sleep but the sandman eluded him. Restless, he fidgeted, turning first one way, then the other. The incessant ticking of the numerous clocks bothered him and with each passing second, their noise seemed to increase. Opening his eyes wide he gazed at an owl clock reflected in the faint light from the window. Its eyes rolled from right to left and Jiminy's eyes also rolled in time with the regular, monotonous tick . . . tock . . . tick . . . tock. Two pendulum clocks swung back and forth, each out of time with the other. Watching their combined movements made Jiminy dizzy. Turning his head in another direction he watched sand falling through an hour-glass. Even that sounded like an anvil striking. Would he never get to sleep?

Angrily reaching for his hat he slammed it down over his head in an endeavour to shut out some of the noise. It wasn't much use. Geppetto and Figaro snored on, blissfully unaware of the disturbance they were creating for a very exasperated cricket. Even Cleo emitted dainty little snores as she blew a froth of bubbles. It was too much! Jiminy jumped to his feet, filled his lungs with air and shouted as loud as he could, 'Quiet!!!' The clocks were stunned into sudden silence . . . even their pendulums remained stationary.

Jiminy nodded his head in satisfaction and removed his hat. 'After all,' he told the room in general, 'enough's enough!' Contentedly, he settled back on the violin, closing his eyes. But what was that? Sharply he turned his head, cocking an inquisitive eye as the light in the room increased. Perplexed, Jiminy jumped to his feet. 'Now what's up?' he asked.

His eyes were riveted on the window. A star was falling through the sky, coming closer and closer, suffusing the room with a brilliant silvery light. Jiminy wasn't waiting around. Grabbing his clothes, he dashed for a hiding place. There was a pipe on the table and Jiminy hopped up and hid inside the bowl, well out of sight. That was one of the advantages of being so small . . . he could hide in the most unlikely places.

The dazzling light entered the room through the open window. Cautiously, Jiminy opened up his umbrella and peered over the pipe bowl. His eyes nearly popped out of his head in surprise. Standing beside the bench where Pinocchio lay, was the most beautiful Blue Fairy. Her long blue dress was of a shiny material and her gauzy wings were a deeper shade of blue. Dainty blue shoes peeked from beneath the hem of her dress and a blue ribbon was threaded through her gleaming gold hair. She had quite the largest, bluest eyes that Jiminy had ever seen. Entranced, he held his breath in awe, wondering what would happen next.

The Blue Fairy stepped lightly towards the bed where Geppetto lay sleeping. Bending over him she said in honeyed tones, 'Good Geppetto, you have given so much happiness to others that you deserve to have your wish come true!' Straightening up, she smiled and walked back to where Pinocchio lay sprawled on the bench. Waving a silver wand she spoke to the puppet:

Little puppet made of pine,
Awake! The gift of life is thine!

Lightly touching him on the head with her
wand, she smiled. A ray of blinding light filled
the room. Slowly it vanished and when Jiminy
Cricket blinked and looked over at the bench,
he saw Pinocchio's strings dissolve. Then the
little wooden puppet began to move, batting his
eyes and rubbing them.

'Whew!' Jiminy topped his hat back on his
head and let his umbrella fall. 'What they can't
do these days!'

Pinocchio was now sitting on the bench. He
turned his head right and left, then waved his
hands in the air. 'I can move!' In consterna-
tion, he clasped his hands across his mouth. 'I
can talk!' Rapidly, he batted his eyes. There
was no end to his wonderment. The Blue Fairy
laughed as she watched. Pinocchio got to his
feet, taking his first unsteady steps. 'I can
walk,' he said then fell down with a clatter and
looked up shyly, blinking his eyes. He would
have to practise.

'Yes, Pinocchio,' answered the Blue Fairy. 'I
have given you life!'

'Why?' asked Pinocchio.

The Blue Fairy stole a glance over at the
sleeping form of Geppetto, 'Because tonight,
Geppetto wished for a real boy!'

'Am I a real boy?'

Jiminy stole quietly along a shelf drawing
closer to the incredible scene unfolding before
his eyes, using the handle of a jug as a temporary hook for his umbrella.

'No, Pinocchio, you are not,' replied the Blue
Fairy. 'To make Geppetto's wish come true will
be entirely up to you!'

Pinocchio pointed to himself and asked
wonderingly, 'Up to me?'

The Blue Fairy looked sweet yet serious.
'Prove yourself brave, truthful, unselfish and

some day you will be a *real* boy!'

Jiminy, listening from the shelf shrugged and muttered, 'That won't be easy!'

Blue Fairy looked all round her then back at Pinocchio. 'You must learn to choose between right and wrong.'

Pinocchio studied first his right hand and then his left. 'Right and wrong?' he said innocently. 'But how will I know?'

Jiminy Cricket threw out his arms in exasperation. 'How will he know!' Jiminy strutted a few steps, puffing out his chest.

'Your conscience will tell you,' replied the Blue Fairy patiently.

'What are conscience?' Pinocchio had a great deal to learn.

Jiminy clapped his hand to his head. 'What are conscience!' he repeated in a tone of exasperation. Suddenly he made up his mind. Using his umbrella as a parachute he sailed through the air, shouting, 'I'll tell you!' He landed on the bench beside a very surprised Pinocchio. 'A conscience,' continued Jiminy, 'is that still, small voice . . . yes, small voice . . . that people won't listen to.' Jiminy hopped onto a match-box, waving his arms in the air. 'That's just the trouble with the world today . . . you see . . .'

'Are you my conscience?' cut in a curious Pinocchio.

'Who . . . me?' Now it was Jiminy's turn to point to himself in amazement.

The Blue Fairy laughed, a sound as lovely as the tinkling of harebells when the wind rustles through them in spring. She leaned close to Jiminy, perched on a match-box, and whispered in his ear. 'Would you like to be Pinocchio's conscience?'

Jiminy's face grew red and he started to squirm. 'Well, uh . . . well . . . I . . . uh uhuh!'

The Blue Fairy laughed understandingly. 'Very well . . . what is your name?'

Jiminy looked up, trying not to feel embarrassed and shy in front of the beautiful creature standing close to him. 'Huh? Oh . . . ah . . . Cricket's the name . . .' Pausing, he tipped his hat. '. . . Jiminy Cricket!' He bowed low.

The Blue Fairy smiled. 'Kneel, Mister Cricket!'

'Huh? Oh!' Jiminy knelt down. 'No tricks, now!'

The Blue Fairy touched Jiminy on each shoulder with her wand, illuminating him in brilliant light. 'I dub you Pinocchio's conscience, Lord High Keeper of Right and Wrong — Counsellor in moments of temptation — guide along the straight and narrow path.' The brilliant light faded. 'Arise! Sir Jiminy Cricket!'

Jiminy rose to his feet, then laughed delightedly. His hat, his umbrella, his suit and shoes were all new . . . brand new. The Blue Fairy had worked her magic again. 'Well, ho, ho, ho.' Jiminy looked down with pride at his shiny shoes. 'My, my . . . say, that's pretty swell!' Proudly he put on his hat, stuck his thumbs beneath the lapels of his coat and twirled round. 'Gee, thanks!' He looked intently at the Blue Fairy. 'But . . . uh . . . don't I get a badge or somethin'?'

The Blue Fairy replied, 'Well, we'll see . . .'

'You mean . . . maybe I will?' Jiminy positively beamed with pride.

'I shouldn't wonder,' laughed the Blue Fairy cordially.

'Make it a gold one?' Jiminy stood on tiptoe on the match-box.

'Maybe!' The Blue Fairy turned to Pinocchio. 'Now, remember, Pinocchio, be a good boy and always let your conscience be your guide.' She stretched her arms in front of her, holding her wand firmly. Gradually she faded into a hazy blue mist, then vanished altogether.

Jiminy swept his hat from his head. 'Goodbye, my lady!' he whispered.

'Goodbye!' echoed Pinocchio from the bench, waving into the empty air.

Jiminy hopped down from the match-box and strolled importantly along a shelf. He felt very dignified in his new outfit. A tall green bottle clearly showed his reflection and he stopped to look at himself and adjust his collar, singing happily, 'La-da-de-da. Not bad, says I . . .' Suddenly Pinocchio's reflection also appeared. Jiminy jumped. 'Oh yeah . . . hah, hah, hah! Almost forgot about you!' He cleared his throat. 'Well, Pinoke . . . maybe you and I had better have a little heart to heart talk!'

'Why?' Pinocchio held out his hands in an expressive gesture.

Jiminy returned to the match-box. It was a little stage from which to deliver advice. 'Well, you want to be a real boy, don't you?'

Pinocchio nodded vigorously. 'Uh-huh!'

'All right! Sit down, son!' Pinocchio sat down with a resounding thud causing the match-box to bounce. Jiminy lifted his coat tails and sat carefully on the box. 'Now, you see,' he began 'the world is full of temptations.'

An expression of surprise crossed Pinocchio's features. 'Temptations?'

'Yep . . . temptations. They're the wrong things that seem right at the time but . . . uh . . . even though things may seem wrong sometimes . . .' Jiminy paused reflectively and picked up his umbrella to help him demonstrate his point, '. . . sometimes the wrong things . . . ha . . . may be right at the wrong time . . . or . . . er . . . vice versa . . . ha, ha!' Jiminy gulped nervously. This wasn't easy. 'Understand?' he asked finally.

Pinocchio started to nod in agreement then changed his mind. 'Uh uh.' He shook his head.

Jiminy Cricket was baffled. He covered his face with his hand. How best could he explain?

'But I'm going to do right!' cut in Pinocchio sincerely.

Jiminy looked relieved. Perhaps he was getting somewhere with his lesson after all. Joyfully he leapt to his feet. 'Atta boy, Pinoke, and

I'm gonna help ya!'

Pinocchio sat down on the floor, Jiminy at his feet. 'And any time you need me . . . you know . . . just whistle? Jiminy gestured, hat in hand. 'Like this!' He whistled, a long, piercing whistle.

Pinocchio inclined his head then drew a deep breath. 'Like this?' Pursing his lips he blew; no sound came out. The little fellow looked disappointed and surprised.

'No, no, try again, Pinoke!'

Pinocchio tried again . . . and again but all his attempts were unsuccessful.

Jiminy shook his head. 'No, son. Now, listen . . . listen to me.' He demonstrated, whistling a jaunty tune.

Pinocchio had another try. At last . . . at last . . . he got it and beamed widely.

'That's it,' said Jiminy, obviously delighted too. 'Come on, now. Let's sing it.' Jumping on to a table, Jiminy sang:

When you get in trouble,
And you don't know what to do,
Give a little whistle,
Give a little whistle.
When you meet temptation
And the urge is very strong,
Give a little whistle,
Give a little whistle.
Not just a little squeak,
Pucker up and blow,
And if your whistle's weak — yell!

'For Jiminy Cricket?' enquired Pinocchio.

'Right!' called Jiminy. 'That's right!' Using the violin strings as a tightrope, he raised his umbrella above his head and walked along, continuing:

Take the straight and narrow path,
And if you start to slide,

Give a little whistle,
Give a little whistle,
And always let your conscience
Be your guide!

Jiminy strutted on the violin bridge. Without warning it snapped, slapped him on the bottom and knocked him into the air. Quickly, with a grin, he picked himself up. He was in high spirits. Next, he imitated a trombone player, bounced onto a clock and using his umbrella, set the clock at the half hour. In answer to his rap on its face the clock door opened and a family of Swiss bell ringers marched out. Jiminy joined them, strutting like a drum major. A model cow and a farm girl both swung bells as the little family returned to their home inside the clock. Jiminy again burst into song:

Take the straight and narrow path,
And if you start to slide,
Give a little whistle,
Yoo hoo!
Give a little whistle.
Woo woo!
And always let your conscience be your guide,
And always let your conscience be your guide!

Pinocchio whirled and danced to the catchy tune. Suddenly, Jiminy yelled a warning. 'Look out, Pinoke!' Too late! Pinocchio tripped over the toy-maker's paint-pots and fell off the shelf. He thudded to the floor and the room seemed to vibrate with the force of his fall. It awoke Geppetto and Figaro. They exchanged looks then peered into the gloom. Cleo also emerged from her castle and peered wide-eyed through her bowl.

'Who is dere?' called Geppetto.

Jiminy dived into a pile of books as Pinocchio answered, 'It's me!'

'Oh, it's me!' repeated Geppetto sleepily,

snuggling down again. Suddenly he shot bolt upright and hopped out of bed. 'Huh?' Raising his fingers to his lips he looked at his cat. 'Shhh ... Figaro!' he warned.

Figaro's back arched and his ears stood straight up in fright. 'There's somebody in here,' said Geppetto peering behind a row of books. Figaro didn't wait to hear more but dived straight under the pillow. Geppetto returned to the side of the bed, struck a match and lit a candle. The flame spluttered, casting long, eerie shadows on the walls. From beneath the mattress he withdrew a blunderbuss. Figaro, feeling ashamed of being a coward, crept guiltily from his hiding place and cautiously followed Geppetto across the room, keeping close to his heels. He got tangled up in his feet and meouwed loudly.

'Shhh! Careful now, Figaro,' cautioned Geppetto. 'He might spring out on us at any time!' The toy-maker peered anxiously in all the corners. He shook his head. 'He's in here ...somewhere!'

Pinocchio, still lying where he had fallen on the floor, leaned over touching Figaro. 'Here I am,' he said. Figaro let out a frightened yell and leapt right up in front of Geppetto's nightshirt. Geppetto jumped in terror and the blunderbuss fired with a loud roar. Jiminy, hiding on a shelf, hastily ducked to avoid the gunshot. All the clocks started swaying from the force of the explosion. On the turkey clock, a model swung an axe; a hunter fired his gun from the hunting clock; a mother spanked her naughty child on another timepiece and the Drunken Man clock fell over. All was chaos and confusion.

Geppetto frowned in bewilderment, scrutinising various objects in the room. His eyes fell on Pinocchio lying on the floor. 'Ohhh! Pinocchio!' Figaro peeped from beneath Geppetto's nightcap where he had finally taken refuge, then clambered down to the floor. Running towards the puppet, he meouwed again. Setting down his candle, the toy-maker picked Pinocchio off the floor. 'How did you get down there?'

'I fell down!' promptly replied the puppet.

Geppetto brushed wood shavings from the marionette's clothes. 'Oh, you did! Hmmmmm...' Then he jumped backward with great surprise. 'Oh! You are talking!'

Very pleased with the effect he was having on Geppetto, Pinocchio nodded his head. 'Uh huh!'

Geppetto couldn't believe it. 'Na ... na ....no!' he said, unconvinced.

Yes! And I can move, too!' To prove his point, Pinocchio gestured with his hands.

Geppetto stood the magic puppet on the bench. How could this be possible? Surely he was dreaming! 'No, no, no . . . you can't. I'm . . . I'm dreaming in my sleep! Wake me up!' Running round the room excitedly, he yelled, 'Wake me up!'

Dashing to the cold water pitcher he ducked his head into it. 'Brrr . . .' He shook the icy water from his face. 'Now we will see who is dreaming.' Figaro shivered and shook icy water from his fur for he had been splashed. Walking back to Pinocchio, Geppetto adjusted his glasses. 'Go on,' he challenged. 'Say something!'

Pinocchio covered his mouth with his hand and snickered. 'Gee! You're funny! Do it again!'

Geppetto's eyes widened with wonder. Wagging his finger at his latest creation, he said, 'You *do* talk!'

Pinocchio nodded enthusiastically, anxious to tell his story. 'Yes! The Blue Fairy came and . . .'

Geppetto leaned forward. 'The Blue Fairy?'

'Uh huh . . . and I've got a conscience!'

Jiminy, still hidden pointed proudly to himself.

'A conscience?' questioned Geppetto.

Pinocchio inclined his head. 'And some day I'm gonna be a *real* boy!'

Geppetto gasped his pleasure then grabbing Pinocchio, swung him in the air. 'A *real* boy! It's . . . it's my wish. It's come true!' Figaro stood on his hind legs, smiling broadly. It delighted him to see his master so happy. 'Figaro,' said Geppetto, 'Why . . . look . . . he's alive, he can talk.' He placed Pinocchio on the floor, close to the cat. 'Say hello to Figaro,' he told the puppet.

'Hello to Figaro!' Pinocchio leaned over to pet him but instinct made Figaro draw back; then he thought better of his action and allowed the puppet to stroke him.

When Geppetto glanced across the room he observed Cleo swimming round and round in her fish bowl. 'Oh . . . oh, Cleo . . . I almost forgot.' Taking Pinocchio by the hand he led him to the table. 'Look,' he said to his pet goldfish. 'It's . . . it's Pinocchio!' Curious, Pinocchio stuck his finger into the bowl. 'She's my little water-baby — isn't she cute?' Cleo swum to the surface of the water.

'Yeah, cute!' answered Pinocchio. Figaro jumped on to the table and both he and Pinocchio peered over the edge of Cleo's bowl. She leapt unexpectedly from the water, kissing Pinocchio on the cheek. He smiled. Cleo decided on an encore; this time she kissed Figaro. Disgusted, the little cat wiped his mouth and turned away. Geppetto roared with laughter as he stroked the silky cat's head. Next he picked up Pinocchio, tossing him high in the air. 'This calls for a celebration!' Carrying the puppet in his arms, Geppetto went into another room and returned minutes later, loaded with an assortment of toys and music-boxes.

'Music, Professor,' he cried loudly, winding up one of the boxes. He wound up a second one. 'Hah, hah, hah! You start one, Pinocchio!'

Filled with confidence, Pinocchio approached a music-box. Figaro sat close to the fish bowl and he and Cleo enjoyed the sweet music. Geppetto and Pinocchio danced and Geppetto sang, 'One, two, three . . . tra la la la drum da . . .' He was happier than he had ever been in his life.

Jiminy Cricket was enjoying the merry spectacle, though he felt rather left out. 'Oh boy, a party!' He stared longingly at dancers in colonial costumes waltzing on top of another music-box. Jiminy came to a swift decision. 'Mind if I cut in?' he asked as he hopped over and took a lady doll in his arms. 'How about sitting this one out, babe — huh?' The doll didn't reply but when Jiminy tried to waltz he found himself in a tangle with the other dancers. Desperately, he struggled to free himself. 'Whoops . . . hey! Whoa . . . let me out . . . let me out!' he cried. The dancers suddenly parted and Jiminy found himself flying through the air. He landed on the floor, slightly stunned.

Geppetto was still dancing. He moved over to Cleo. 'Come, Cleo . . . join the party . . . dance!' Plunging his hand into the water he stirred it round. Cleo pirouetted while Geppetto continued singing.

'Ohh . . . nice!' murmured Pinocchio, loving the excitement. He glanced at a candle burning beside him and because he liked the flame, he tried to lift it from the candle. Figaro jumped up to watch while Geppetto sang, his arms overflowing with toys.

Tra la la la . . . gathering toys,
Tra la la, for my little boy . . .

Tentatively, Figaro stretched out his paw towards the candle flame and Pinocchio plunged his finger right into it. His finger started to burn and he held it in the air. 'Look . . . pretty!' he said.

Geppetto looked in the boy's direction. 'Yes . . . pretty,' he agreed, then realised what was happening. 'Oh, help,' he yelled. Pinocchio raised his finger high above his head watching the flames change colour. Distracted, Geppetto seized him and attempted to blow out the flame. His breath fanned it into stronger life. 'Wh . . . wh . . . where's the bucket?' he gasped dashing across the room. 'Help! Water! Where's the water?' Figaro, also alarmed, got under his feet and let out a loud yell as Geppetto accidentally trod on his tail.

Quick-thinking Jiminy filled his hat with water and rushed forward. 'Here it is . . . I've got it. Here's water! Here's some water! Oomph!' A pencil lay in his path and Jiminy in his urgent rush tripped head first and fell into his own hat of water. In the general uproar, Jiminy's efforts hadn't been noticed. Geppetto was still crying, 'Help! Water! Water!' Rushing over to the fish bowl he plunged Pinocchio's finger into the liquid. The burning finger sizzled — then the flame died as the water clouded over.

'That was close.' Geppetto gently massaged the injured finger. 'Maybe we'd better go to bed before something else happens.'

Cleo rose to the surface of her bowl, exhaling smoke rings. She felt a little burned-up at Pinocchio's careless behaviour.

At last an air of peace and calm descended over the room. It was time for everyone to settle down. Jiminy yawned. 'Ho hum,' he said, hopping upon the match-box. 'Little man, you've had a busy night!' Kicking off his shoes, he made up a bed inside the match-box then pulled over the cover, turned on his side and closed his eyes. It was time for a cricket to catch up on his sleep.

Minutes later, Geppetto, Pinocchio and Figaro were all snug in the toy-maker's bed. Geppetto extinguished the candle and put his arm around Pinocchio. 'Now, close your eyes and go to sleep,' he told him.

'Why?' questioned Pinocchio, struggling to sit up.

Figaro, wearing a tiny night cap on his furry head, opened one eye. How could anyone question the luxury of a nap . . . even a catnap!

Geppetto explained. 'Oh, everybody has to sleep — Figaro goes to sleep, and Cleo and besides, tomorrow you've got to go to school.'

Pinocchio opened his eyes very wide. 'Why?'

Figaro, exasperated at constant questions and answers, angrily tossed his covers aside and glared at Pinocchio.

'Oh,' said Geppetto patiently, 'to learn things and get smart.'

Figaro pulled a face and ducked beneath a pillow. 'Why?' repeated Pinocchio. 'Oh . . . because . . .' Geppetto's voice grew more and more drowsy. His eyes drooped, then he fell fast asleep.

'Ohhh!' said Pinocchio. With no one to talk to he lay down, closed his eyes and floated away like the others to Dreamland.

CHAPTER THREE

The following morning was clear and bright. Great clouds billowed in snowy splendour across an azure sky and from the church tower, a bell tolled. Already the narrow cobbled streets were alive with the sound of children's voices, their happy laughter floating on the air as they played games. A boy dashed from his house to the water trough and drank deeply; two others playing leap-frog called out to him. Across the ancient rooftops, pigeons flew in ever widening circles. At night they roosted in the tower but each morning when the bell started tolling, they flew into the trees or settled on window-ledges.

The toy-maker's house was also a scene of lively excitement. Geppetto hadn't previously known the pleasure of sending his very own little boy off to school and it was an exhilarating experience. The front door of the cottage opened and Geppetto, Pinocchio and Figaro stepped onto the ancient grey stone porch. Pinocchio and the little cat began to play games and Geppetto smiled at their antics. Over his arm, he carried Pinocchio's coat.

'Oh, look, father, look!' Pinocchio pointed but Geppetto was not paying attention. 'What are those?' insisted Pinocchio.

Geppetto was forced to look up. 'Huh! Oh,

those . . . they are your schoolmates! Girls and boys. There! Now get into this!' At last he managed to get Pinocchio into his coat.

Pinocchio wasn't interested in clothes at the moment. He asked curiously, *'Real* boys?'

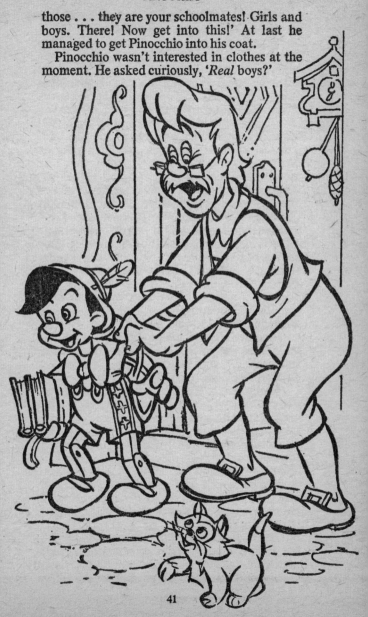

'Yes! But hurry now . . .' Pinocchio dashed eagerly into the street, anxious to mingle with the other children. 'Oh, wait, wait, wait!' cried Geppetto. Pinocchio looked over his shoulder and saw Geppetto taking an apple from his pocket. He polished it on his sleeve, then handed it to Pinocchio. 'Here's an apple for the teacher. Now turn round and let me look you over!' Geppetto inspected him, then chuckled. Pinocchio looked very smart, a credit to him. Feeling a brushing motion against his leg he looked down. Figaro was meouwing and tugging a book on to the porch. 'Huh? Oh, yeah . . . yes, uh . . . here!' Geppetto picked up the book and handed it to Pinocchio. 'Uhhuh, run along now!' There was love and infinite tenderness in the kindly toy-maker's voice as he watched the little creature skip gaily along the pavement.

Figaro chased after him leaping and gambolling as he ran. 'Ho, ho, ho, wait . . . wait . . . come back here, Figaro! School is not for you!' Geppetto ran on to the cobbles and picked up his furry pet.

Together, they watched Pinocchio running away into the distance, clutching his book in one hand, his apple in the other. At the corner he turned, calling 'Goodbye, Father!'

'Goodbye, son,' called Geppetto and waved. 'Hurry back!' Cheerily, Geppetto turned round and danced his way indoors.

All the children made their way towards the school-house. Some hurried . . . some dallied. Their various antics were being observed by a cunning fox and a large cat, who were concealed in an old passage-way. 'Ah, Gideon,' said the fox whose real name was J. Worthington Foulfellow but who was known as Honest John, 'listen to the merry laughter of innocent children wending their way to school.' He swung his cane in the direction of the boys and girls.

Gideon grimaced. School held no appeal for

him. 'Thirsty little minds rushing to the fountain of knowledge . . . ha ha!' He stopped speaking to spear a cigar lying on the pavement. His cane came in very useful for such things. 'School,' he went on as he removed the cigar, 'is a noble institution.' He took a match from his pocket, preparing to light his find. 'What would this stupid world be without . . .' He paused and started in surprise as his crafty eyes alighted on a poster. 'Well, well, well . . .' He crossed the street to study it at close range. The poster read: 'The Great Stromboli — Marionette Show.' Honest John laughed. 'Stromboli — so that old rascal's back in town, eh! Remember, Giddy, the time I tied strings to you and passed you off as a puppet?' Giddy nodded, looking bashful. He did not care to be reminded of that particular incident.

Honest John swished his red bushy tail. 'Ah, we nearly put one over on the old gypsy that time!' He guffawed loudly at the memory, well pleased with his trick. At that precise moment, Pinocchio skipped in between Honest John and Gideon, a sweet smile of anticipation on his face. He was looking forward to his first day of school and mixing with real, live children.

'Hmmm . . .' commented Honest John. 'A little wooden boy. Ha, ha, hum . . . now who ev . . .' He stopped speaking and jumped high in the air. Both surprise and excitement were contained in his sudden action. *A wooden boy!!!* he repeated. Gideon and the fox stared hard at Pinocchio's retreating figure. 'Look, Giddy, look!' cried the wily fox. 'It's amazing . . . a live puppet without strings!' His crafty green eyes narrowed as he stroked his chin. His mind was working overtime. 'A thing like that ought to be worth a fortune to someone . . . now let me see . . .' He jerked up. 'That's it! That's it!' He pointed enthusiastically to the Stromboli poster. 'Stromboli! Why, that . . . that old fakir would give us . . . listen!' Standing close to Gideon he whispered in his furry ear. Gideon's eyes lit up with glee — and greed. One could almost see the dollar signs reflected in his orbs. Honest John rubbed the palms of his hands and licked his lips. This was the best piece of luck that had crossed the two scoundrels' paths for some time.

'If we play our cards right, cackled the fox, 'we'll be on easy street . . . or my name isn't Honest John!'

Gideon nodded his wholesale approval. 'Quick!' urged the fox. 'We will head him off!'

Pinocchio, completely unaware of the interest he had aroused, hurried blithely towards the school-house. The cat and the fox concealed themselves from Pinocchio's view by ducking behind a wall, but gradually drew

closer. Gideon had helped himself to a flower-
pot from a doorstep as he passed. He felt it
might come in useful for something, though he
wasn't sure just what. Because he was lagging,
Honest John's cane jerked him forward

knocking the flower pot to the ground. To Giddy's indignation it smashed into a hundred pieces. The fox kept the cane wrapped round the cat's neck. At such an important moment, he wasn't taking chances on tardy behaviour from his partner.

Honest John peered through an archway. 'Shhhh!' he admonished. 'Now's our . . .' He looked over his shoulder. Gideon was no longer attached to the cane. He frowned. Now where the deuce . . . Giddy suddenly appeared beside him, a mallet raised above his head. Clearly it was his intention to strike poor Pinocchio a mighty blow on the head when he drew near.

'No, no, stupid!' Honest John grabbed the mallet, pushing Giddy on to the cobbles with a thud. 'Don't be crude!' he admonished. 'Let me handle this.' He squinted along the street. 'Here he comes.'

Placing himself directly in Pinocchio's path he spoke to the goggle-eyed Gideon. 'Ah yes, Giddy, as I was saying to the Duchess only yesterday . . .' As the little puppet drew level with the conspirators, the fox deliberately tripped him with his cane. Pinocchio sprawled on the ground. Immediately, Honest John rushed to his assistance, feigning sympathy. 'Oh, oh!' he said in distressed tones while helping the startled boy to his feet. 'How clumsy of me.' With a great show of concern he brushed dust from Pinocchio's clothes. 'Oh, my, my, my! Let me adjust your tie and hat. Tsk, tsk, tsk . . . oh, I'm terribly sorry!'

Giddy pulled his jacket aside and produced a whisk broom from an inner pocket. The cat brushed Pinocchio's pants. 'Oh, I do hope you are not injured,' went on Honest John.

'I'm all right,' answered a rather dazed Pinocchio.

Giddy, never one to miss an opportunity, attempted to pick the little puppet's pockets. Swift as lightning, Honest John's cane rapped him sharply. Blinking stupidly, Gideon picked himself up from the pavement.

Honest John turned back to Pinocchio with a suave smile. 'Ah, splendid! I'm so glad that you're not hurt.' He picked up Pinocchio's apple and book from the cobbles, glancing at the book's cover. 'Well, well ... hmmmmm ... quite a scholar, I see.' He turned to Giddy who was still seeing a multitude of stars. 'Look, Giddy, a man of letters!' Giddy shook his head in an effort to clear away the misty haze in front of his eyes.

'Here's your book!' With a display of gallantry, Honest John handed it over.

'I'm going to school,' said Pinocchio proudly. Turning on his heel he started off again ... but he didn't get far.

'School . . . ah, yes!' The fox jerked Pinocchio backwards, using his cane. 'Then you haven't heard of the easy road to success.' He put his arms round Pinocchio's shoulders and took a bite out of the luscious rosy apple Pinocchio held in his hand.

'Uh-uh!' Pinocchio shook his head.

'No?' Honest John took the apple and bit deeply into it. 'I'm speaking, my boy, of the theatre.' Assuming a dramatic pose he drew his cloak about him.

Pinocchio's innocent eyes widened in wonder. Honest John finished the apple and returned the core to the puppet. 'Here's your apple.' Pinocchio frowned at the brown core. Honest John continued talking. 'Bright lights ... music ... applause ... *Fame!*'

Pinocchio raised his eyebrows. 'Fame?'

'Yes . . .' Honest John clasped his hands together pretending to be very impressed with Pinocchio's charms. 'And with that personality, that profile, that physique, why ...' He glanced swiftly in Giddy's direction. 'Why, he's a natural born actor, eh, Giddy!' Giddy nodded.

'But I'm going straight to ...' insisted Pinocchio still endeavouring once more to follow the children. He didn't want to be late on his first morning — and now, he didn't have his apple for teacher.

Pinocchio's path was blocked by the very determined fox. He swished his cane. 'Why . . . I can see your name in lights,' insisted the scoundrel. 'Lights six feet high . . . uh . . . what is your name?'

'Pinocchio!'

'Pinocchio,' repeated Honest John and started to spell it out, letter by letter. He raised his finger. 'We are wasting precious time! Come — on to the theatre!'

Almost before Pinocchio was aware of what was happening, he found himself being marched through the cobbled streets in the opposite direction to the school-house. The fox walked jubilantly on one side of him, Gideon padded along on the other. As they strolled, Honest John twirled his cane and sang:

Hi diddle dee dee,
An actor's life for me.
A high silk hat and a silver cane,
A watch of gold with a diamond chain,
Hi diddle dee day,
An actor's life is gay,
It's great to be a celebrity,
An actor's life for me!

The trio ran round and round a tree, then set off down the road again, Honest John still singing.

Back in Geppetto's cottage, Jiminy Cricket woke up with a start. He had overslept. Pinocchio had already left for school so Jiminy flung his clothes on, fixed his tie and put his shiny new hat on his head. 'Whoo . . . fine conscience I turned out to be,' he told his reflection in the green bottle which he used as a mirror. 'Late the first day.' He buttoned his vest, tucked in his shirt and hurried from the toy-maker's house. 'Oh well,' mused the cricket, hurrying down the street, 'he can't get in much trouble between here and school!'

Hopping on to the edge of the wall he scanned the pavement with his sharp eyes. Was that a procession in the distance? He jumped behind a wall. 'Oh boy — a parade!' he chortled.

Along the street came Honest John, Gideon and Pinocchio. 'Hi diddle dee, an actor's life for me . . .' Jiminy, twirling his umbrella started in surprise when he heard Honest John's words. And surely that was Pinocchio's voice joining in! 'Huh?' he questioned, jumping back on the wall.

Honest John sang a different lyric:

A waxed moustache and a beaver coat,
A pony cart and a billy goat . . .
Hi diddle dee dum,
An actor's life is fun . . .

Jiminy stared in disbelief. 'Why . . . it's Pinoke!' He raced towards the little boy. 'Hey,' he called. 'Where you goin'?'

No one paid any attention, or perhaps they didn't even hear. Honest John was showing off his deep baritone voice:

> You wear your hair in a pompadour,
> You ride around in a coach and four,
> You stop and buy out a candy store,
>   An actor's life for me!

'Hold on there!' Jiminy chased after the trio. Deciding on desperate action, he hopped onto the fox's tail. 'Pinoke!' he called.

Honest John was in full voice this morning. Recklessly, Jiminy hopped on to Honest John's hat, struggling to keep his balance. 'Hey! Pinoke . . . hey!' He whistled shrilly.

> Hi diddle dee doom,
> You sleep 'til after . . .

Honest John paused. 'What was that?' he asked.

Pinocchio glanced up at the fox and noticed the cricket sitting on his hat. 'Oh, it's Jiminy! Whatcha doin' up there?' he asked.

Honest John stared at Pinocchio. 'Huh? Who? What? Jiminy? Up where?'

Giddy spotted Jiminy so the cricket held his fingers to his lips. 'Shhh!' he cautioned.

'Why . . . why, my boy, you must be seeing things!' The fox was very puzzled.

With a wide grin, Giddy 'Shhh'd' back to Jiminy but the artful cat took his mallet from the inside pocket of his coat.

Honest John was still frowning. 'Oh no, I'm not seeing things,' went on Pinocchio. 'He's my conscience . . . he . . .'

Giddy crept round behind Honest John, the mallet ready in his hand. Honest John rubbed his chin, while he talked to Pinocchio. 'Now,

now, now . . . just calm down . . . why, there's nothing up there to be afraid of. Nothing at all!'

Pinocchio's eyes widened as Giddy raised the mallet high, then brought it down with all his strength. Fortunately for Jiminy he saw it coming and hopped out of the way. Honest John fell to the ground with the force of the blow and Giddy on top of him. Giddy picked himself up, a surprised expression on his sneaky face. Honest John lay in a heap on the cobbles, his face buried inside his hat. From its depths came furious mutterings. Giddy, frightened out of his wits knowing Honest John's wrath, looked round for a scapegoat. Handing the mallet to Pinocchio he dashed out of reach.

Jiminy had jumped into the heart of a flower and was viewing the scene from comparative safety. 'Pssssst! Pinoke!' He whistled to attract attention. 'Pinoke, over here!'

Pinocchio walked towards the cricket but when Honest John yelled angrily, Pinocchio hesitated. Jiminy called urgently, 'Woo hoo! Over here!'

Pinocchio stood uncertainly beside the flower talking to Jiminy. 'Oh, Jiminy, I'm going to be an actor!'

Jiminy nodded and raised his hand in the air. 'All right, my son, take it easy now. Remember what I said about temptation?.'

Pinocchio's mouth dropped open. 'Uh — huh!'

Jiminy twirled his umbrella in the direction of the fox. 'Well, that's him!'

Pinocchio shook his head in disbelief. 'Oh no, Jiminy . . . that's Mr. Honest John!'

Jiminy could hardly believe his ears. If the little fellow really thought the fox was honest, it was a catastrophe. 'Honest John? Huh!' he snorted.

The fox was still lying on the ground struggling to remove his hat. It remained firmly wedged over his face and his anger increased with each passing second. Giddy watched in fear, biting his nails in anxiety. There would be the devil to pay once he was free. An idea occurred to the cat. Picking up Honest John's cane he attempted to pry the hat off. It didn't work. He tried the mallet . . . with unfortunate results. Honest John received another mighty whack and this time the fox flew through the air and landed against the trunk of a tree. 'Ohhhhhhh!!!' he screeched. The ground around the base of the tree was wet and very slippery. Honest John slid downwards — right into a pool of water. Drenched and spluttering with fury he sat up and shook himself. The force with which he had struck the tree had accomplished one important thing . . . his hat was knocked off.

Jiminy leaned closer to Pinocchio. At all costs he must try to safeguard the boy from the wily fox. 'All right then,' he said, 'here's what

we'll tell 'em. You can't go to the theatre . . .
say thank you just the same,' he raised his hat
in a gesture of politeness. 'You're sorry, but
you've got to go to school.' Jiminy pointed in
the direction of the school-house with his
umbrella.

'Uh huh!' commented Pinocchio, agreeing
with Jiminy at last.

'Pinocchiooooo!! Oh, Pinocchiooooo! Yoo
hoo!' Honest John and Gideon were walking
towards the little boy. They were crossing a
bridge by the pool for they had no intention of
allowing their future prosperity to escape.

Jiminy, concealed inside the flower shook his
finger in warning. 'Here they come, Pinoke!
Now you can tell 'em.'

Honest John approached with a wheedling
smile on his crafty face. 'Woo hoo! Oh, little
boy! Ah, there you are!' Pinocchio grinned up
at him. 'Where were we?' asked the fox. 'Ah,
yes . . . on to the theatre.'

'Goodbye, Jiminy — goodbye!' Pinocchio
turned briefly in the direction of the flower then
walked away between the cat and the scheming
fox. His promises to Jiminy had been quickly
forgotten.

'Goodbye . . . huh?' Jiminy's forehead
wrinkled in concern. With a deep sense of
shock he realised what was happening.
Pinocchio had no thoughts of going to school,
after all.

Hi diddle dee dee,
An actor's life for me
A silk hat and a silver cane . . .

The fox's voice was back in tune at the
prospect of vast wealth.

'Hey! Pinoke, you can't go . . . uh . . . there
he goes!' Jiminy's cry ended in a wail of
despair.

Honest John's voice floated through the clear
morning air falling like the knell of doom on
Jiminy's ears.

A watch of gold with a diamond chain
Hi diddle dee day
An actor's life is gay

'Oh, what'll I do?' pondered Jiminy. 'I'll run and tell his father.' He jumped down from the flower and hopped in the direction of Geppetto's cottage. Suddenly he stopped. 'No,' he said aloud. 'That would be snitchin'! I'll go after him myself!'

STROMBOLI

CHAPTER FOUR

On that same evening, the theatre where Stromboli was appearing with his famous marionettes was packed. There wasn't a spare seat in the house. People jostled each other as they struggled to reach their appointed places. Red velvet curtains hid the stage as the crowds clapped, impatient for the show to commence. The ceiling was painted rose pink and from it hung a dozen lamps that gave out a soft firefly shimmer. Jiminy Cricket was perched on one of the lamps, as anxious as anyone for the entertainment to start.

The lights dimmed and a hush of expectancy fell over the audience. The curtains parted with a flourish to reveal Stromboli standing on the stage. Jiminy Cricket stared hard. Stromboli was a man who would attract stares. Stocky and thickset, he had a swarthy skin, a bald head and an enormous jet black beard which flowed down to his chest. Large pop-eyes and a hooked nose gave him an ominous appearance. His taste was dazzling. Over his ivory-coloured shirt he wore a bright green waistcoat, an orange cummerbund was swathed about his waist above canary yellow trousers, and his socks and slippers were also orange. He reminded Jiminy of an oversized, flamboyant parrot. After a brief announcement, Stromboli grinned an evil grin, waited for an ovation, then retired amidst applause.

One after another the various marionettes came onto the stage and went through their performances. But at long last came the announcement that Jiminy had been waiting for. Stromboli strutted onto the stage and gestured with his massive hands. 'Ladies and gentlemens, to conclude the performance of this great show, Stromboli, the master showman, that's a me . . .' and he pointed to himself, '. . . and by special permission of the management . . . that's a me too . . . is presenting to you sometin' you will absolutely refuse to believe!'

Jiminy was fast becoming impatient. His perch left much to be desired. Moths were dive-bombing him and it was pretty hot, too. He batted at the moths with his umbrella, then gazed down at the crowd. 'Well, looks like a sell-out!'

Stromboli assumed a dramatic pose, puffing out his chest beneath the expanse of sooty beard. 'Introducing the only marionette who can sing and dance . . . absolutely without the aids of strings!' His speech delivered, he clasped his hands across his protruding tummy and looked skywards. He waved his arms. 'I give you — the one and only Pinocchio!'

The crowd applauded wildly while Jiminy looked down in disgust. 'Huh — what a build up!' he sniffed.

Stromboli stepped into the pit to conduct the orchestra, trumpet-playing puppets appeared and a second curtain rose to reveal Pinocchio standing at the top of a flight of steps. A spotlight was turned upon him and the audience clapped loudly as encouragement. As Pinocchio walked down the stairs he sang: 'I got no strings to hold me da . . .' He lurched and was precipitated forward. He had tripped and the fall landed him on the stage. His nose caught in a knot hole in one of the wooden boards. The crowd roared with enthusiasm thinking it was all a part of the act. Pinocchio looked around and blinked. He couldn't get up.

Jiminy sighed his annoyance. 'Go ahead,' he muttered. 'Make a fool of yourself . . . then maybe you'll listen to your conscience.'

Stromboli was red with anger. His special act had misfired within the first few seconds. Muttering beneath his breath he reached over from the pit and slapped the board viciously off Pinocchio's nose. Then he told him off with great indignation. The crowd smiled understandingly and Stromboli, quick to react to their mood, changed his attitude, patting the little fellow on the head and giving him a few words of encouragement. It had the desired effect. The audience screamed their approval. 'Heh! Heh! Cute kid!' murmured Stromboli, ever the showman.

Pinocchio looked scared standing in the spotlight. Raising one foot, he scratched his other leg with it. The few seconds gave him the necessary time to recover his nerve. He carried on with his song:

> I got no strings to hold me down,
> To make me fret or make me frown,
> I had strings but now I'm free . . .
> There are no strings on me!
> Heigh ho the merry-o
> That's the only way to be
> I want the world to know
> Nothing ever worries me!

Coyly, he swung his foot and hung his head. The crowd cheered, Stromboli nodded with pleasure. 'What I told you, huh? Ha, ha, ha, ha!'

Pinocchio, a little puzzled at the enthusiasm of the audience shrugged and went on:

> So I have fun and
> I'm not tied up to anyone,
> They've got no strings

But you can see
There are no strings
On me! Whee!

He began to feel a little tired but brightened considerably at the rousing response from the laughing crowds. They liked him — there was no doubt of that. They really liked him.

The spotlight went out and the footlights came on. From overhead, a Dutch girl puppet dropped into the scene. She was very pretty and wore a tiny bonnet on her blonde plaits and a sweet blue and white gingham dress. Her clogs had flowers painted on them. She drew close to Pinocchio, a smile on her pink and white face and began to sing to him:

You haff no strings,
Your arms is free,
To lüff me by the Zuider Zee.
Ya ya ya . . .
If you would woo
I'd boost my strings for you.

On the word 'boost' the little Dutch puppet leapt into the air and Pinocchio jumped with her in surprise. A chorus of similarly attired Dutch dolls appeared and performed a clog dance. Pinocchio became sandwiched between the dancers and was just wondering whatever he should do when the Dutch curtain dropped . . . and a French puppet appeared.

She too, was pretty and with a provocative movement she sidled over to Pinocchio. Pinocchio gazed at the new arrival with awe. She was very chic and batted her eyelashes at him as she sang:

You've got no strings
Comme ci, comme ça,
Your savoir faire is
ooh, lala . . .
I've got no strings,
But entre nous sa,
I'd cut my strings for you!

Stepping right up to him she flung her arms around the startled Pinocchio. It was her cue to vanish and as she did so, a French dancing chorus appeared in her place. The music's pace quickened as they danced the Can Can with joy and gusto.

Jiminy, who had been watching the stage in disgust, leaned forward with renewed interest. Quickly snapping on his spectacles he ogled the pretty dancers. When their act was over the lights changed again and this time an attractive Russian girl puppet stepped onto the stage. Dressed in a colourful Russian costume, she had long, dark flowing hair and moved with the speed and grace of a gazelle. Leaping to Pinocchio's side she sang:

> Down vere da Volga flows
> Dere's a Roosian Rendezvous
> Vere me und Ivan go
> But I'd rather go vid you. Hey!

The puppet pivoted and danced across the stage and Pinocchio made a move to follow but she was dramatically whisked from sight. A chorus of very lively Russian dancers followed in her wake, jumping, dancing and shouting 'hey!' at regular intervals. Pinocchio, very intrigued, watched the performers, keeping well out of the way. After a while he attempted to imitate their brilliant style of dancing, pivoting round with folded arms. He started spinning . . . spinning . . . spinning . . . until he became dizzy and got tangled up with the chorus. Blinking, he popped his head above the other puppets, calling out, 'There are no strings on me!' The audience clapped and whistled in appreciation. Pinocchio ducked back with the chorus then fell down, his nose again buried in the theatre boards. A Russian hat skimmed through the air and landed on his head.

When he finally managed to struggle to his feet, a part of the floor board stuck to his nose, resembling a small brown beard. Pinocchio, stunned and still dizzy, gazed at the audience. This was their opportunity to show him how they loved his performance. Rising to their feet they clapped and clapped until their hands ached. They whistled, sang, stomped, flung money and flowers on to the stage. Pinocchio had won their hearts.

Jiminy, still swinging on a lampshade, was overwhelmed at such a reception. It was magnificent — it was incredible. 'Huh! They like him,' he murmured, 'He's a real success!' Removing his hat he scratched his head. 'Gosh! Maybe I was wrong!'

Stromboli strode onto the stage to take his share of the credit, holding an armful of puppets. He fondly stroked Pinocchio on the head — he could afford to show a generous gesture now. His beaming smile grew even broader as more and more coins were flung at Pinocchio's feet. The curtains closed, but the audience wouldn't leave the theatre. Continued applause had torn the curtains apart another three times before the public finally started to meander out onto the cobbled streets and discuss the 'boy miracle.' There had never been such a night in the village.

Jiminy had waited for the first two curtain-calls then hopped from his hot perch and out of the theatre. He was glad to be out into the cool night air for he was reeling from the heat and noise. Thoughtfully, he moved away from the theatre lights. 'Well,' he said aloud, 'I guess he won't need me any more. What does an actor want with a conscience anyway?' His shoulders sagged — he couldn't suppress a feeling of disappointment. Pinocchio no longer needed his services — his advice. Rain began to fall. Jiminy hunched his shoulders and put up his umbrella.

Geppetto was very worried. The long dark

shadows of night clung to the winding streets and his beloved Pinocchio had not returned from school. The other village children had arrived home long before darkness descended. The kindly toy-maker was very distressed. He had made frequent journeys to look for the little boy and now he had set a lighted candle in the window and left the curtains undrawn so that the light would act as a guide. Rain slashed against the panes and the wind moaned fretfully around the house.

The stout wooden table was set for four. Figaro and Cleo were already at the table, both hungry and anxious to start their meal. Figaro had a white linen napkin tied about his neck and on a plate in front of him was an appetising portion of his favourite steamed fish. His nose crinkled as he sniffed the delicious aroma wafting in the air.

Geppetto shook his head and frowned. 'What could have happened to him?' he asked for the twelfth time. 'Where could he be?'

Cleo swam around in her bowl, her eyes fixed on the tempting cake tied on a string just above her head. She felt very hungry tonight.

'Not home at this hour?' Geppetto stood uncertainly at the window, then made up his mind. Crossing to his old-fashioned coatstand he took down his coat and slipped it on. 'I'd better go out again and look for him.' He turned towards the table. 'And remember . . . nobody eats a bite until I find him.'

Solemnly, Figaro and Cleo shook their heads. The toy-maker picked up a lantern and walked out into the cold, wet night. As the door closed, Figaro rubbed his paws in glee and opened his mouth wide to take a bite of fish. Cleo blew a series of bubbles in silent chastisement, then waggled her fin. Figaro looked at her with a guilty expression. He knew he was beaten; sadly he licked his chops and glared straight ahead. Where had Pinocchio got to? Dismally, he settled down to wait.

CHAPTER FIVE

Shortly after the crowds had dispersed, Stromboli closed the theatre and returned to his wagon, located on the edge of the village. Pinocchio trudged along by his side. The marionette master's high spirits were not in the least dampened by the rain ... never had he experienced such an excellent night for business. His takings were astounding and if the coffers continued to fill in similar style, very soon he would be a wealthy man. He sang lustily as he unlocked the wagon door:

> I gotta no strings,
> But I gotta da brain,
> I buya new suit and
> Swinga da cane ...
> I eatta da best and
> I drinka champagne!

Inside the wagon he spread the wealth of coins across a plain deal table. From a cupboard he took bread, cheese and pickles for a meal. He sat down heavily, ready to eat and count his money. Pinocchio felt lonely and clambered onto the table, seating himself on the loaf of bread. Stromboli ignored him ... he was spearing pickles and cheese with a long-bladed, exceedingly sharp knife.

Every now and again he sang gleefully, 'I gotta no strings on me!'

He laughed heartily, his great belly heaving like a mass of jelly, as he turned towards Pinocchio. 'Bravo, Pinocchio,' he said as he speared more food on the end of his knife.

'They liked me!' commented Pinocchio wistfully.

'Ummmmmmmm!' Stromboli's mind wasn't so much on the boy as the stack of coins piled up in front of him. Using the tip of his knife he counted aloud. 'Two hundred . . .' He paused. 'You are sensational!' He speared an olive as Pinocchio smiled.

'You mean I'm good?' he asked.

'Ah . . . three hundred . . .' Stromboli placed the coins with the other counted stacks. 'You are colossal!' Unexpectedly, and with terrific force, he brought the knife down through the loaf of bread on which Pinocchio was seated. Both Pinocchio and the bread bounced. Stromboli speared a hunk of the bread and an onion.

After Pinocchio had recovered from shock he whispered in a small voice, 'Does this mean I'm an actor?'

'Sure!' Stromboli bit into the onion, pushed back his chair and stood up — a rotund, brightly clad, menacing figure. 'I will poosh you in the public's eye . . . your face, she will be on everybody's tongue!' Seizing Pinocchio by the head he held him high in the air. With a coarse laugh he dropped him back on the table.

Trembling, Pinocchio picked himself up, tears filling his eyes. He was badly frightened. 'Will she?' he asked in a tiny voice.

'Yeah!' Stromboli sounded indifferent. Pinocchio's distress didn't worry the callous man in the least. His ugly face suddenly darkened, like a black thunder-cloud. He had discovered a bad coin amongst the hoard. 'Ahuh! What's dis?' Angrily he tested the coin by biting its edge. 'Filthy cheats!'

3

he shrieked as he flung it on the floor. 'I make somebody paya for theés!' An idea struck him. Bending down, he retrieved the coin and placed it in Pinocchio's hand. 'For you . . . my little Pinocchio!'

Pinocchio was sitting on the edge of the table. 'For me? Gee, thanks!' He got to his feet. 'I'll run home and tell my father.'

Stromboli, greedily guzzling wine from a bottle almost choked when he heard Pinocchio's words. 'Home?' he roared, then burst into cruel, raucous laughter. 'Oh . . . ho, ho, ho . . . sure. Going home to your father!' He lowered himself into a chair. Trembling with mirth he fell across the table, tears streaming from his eyes. 'Oh, that is very comeecal!'

Pinocchio was looking puzzled. 'You mean it's funny?'

Stromboli wiped the tears from his fat cheeks. 'Sure. Yeah!'

Pinocchio shrugged then raised his hat. In a quiet, determined voice he said, 'I'll be back in the morning!'

Stromboli abruptly stopped laughing. His expression changed into one of menace. 'Be back in the morning?' he muttered beneath his breath as Pinocchio jumped down from the table. 'Going home?' he asked smoothly, inclining his grotesque head and wagging his finger. He laughed again . . . a low, threatening sound. Uncertainly, Pinocchio joined in the laughter.

Suddenly, Stromboli seized the unsuspecting Pinocchio and flung him roughly into a cage and slammed the door. Then he padlocked it. 'This will be your home,' the terrible man shouted, '. . . where I can always find you.' In the background, dozens of puppets swung from their strings, covering the walls of Stromboli's wagon. Pinocchio was just as helpless now as they were. The cage in which he was imprisoned was round with very strong metal bars. It swung from an overhead hook. Pinocchio, terrified out of his wits, struggled to his feet. He grabbed the bars, trying to force them. 'No! No! No!' he cried desperately.

'Yes! Yes! Yes!' answered Stromboli. 'To me you are belonging.' He beat his chest with his huge fists shouting, 'We will tour the world! Paris ... London ... Monte Carlo ... Constantinople!'

'No! No!' screamed Pinocchio in terror.

Stromboli clenched his fist and pounded on the table until it vibrated beneath the force of his blows. 'Yes! We start tonight!' Scooping the piles of coins into a money-bag he said villainously, 'Ummmmmmm! You are my gold-mine — my securities for the future! You will make lots of money for me.' Greedily he caressed the bulging money-bag, then his black brows furrowed and he seized an axe from a nearby shelf. 'And when you are growing too old ...' he paused to moisten his thumb and wet the sharp blade of the axe, '... then you will make good *firewood!*' After delivering these terrifying words, Stromboli flung the axe into a wood box containing discarded puppets ready for burning. The axe struck one of them causing it to quiver pathetically. Stromboli flung back his head and bellowed with amusement. He was on to a good thing. He couldn't lose. His transaction earlier that day with Honest John was going to pay off handsomely.

Refusing to accept defeat, Pinocchio struggled with the bars, shouting and pleading, 'Lemme outta here ... I gotta get out ... you can't keep me!'

Stromboli, angered at the boy's defiant spirit jumped in the air. As he landed, the entire floor of the wagon shook and everything else vibrated. *'Quiet!'* he yelled in a deafening voice. 'Belt up before I knocka you seely!'

Pinocchio's face crumpled. It seemed as though he was beaten. Stromboli noticed the expression of defeat. His cunning mind realised that it would be wiser to be nice to the trapped boy . . . as long as it suited his own scheming ends. Wiping the black, thunderous look from his face he replaced it with a faint smile. He blew Pinocchio a kiss. 'Good night . . . my leetle wooden gold-mine!' Mockingly, he bowed, then went out of the room.

Pinocchio started to struggle again with the unyielding bars. 'No . . . wait! Lemme out!' He shook his little fist. 'I'll tell my father!' he shouted, but Stromboli had vanished.

Later, he re-appeared, a disagreeable smirk on his face. He swung the cage so that it spun dizzily. 'Tch tch tch . . . git along there!' he mocked before going out to climb on the front of the wagon. It was time to be on the move; there was no point in hanging around until daylight. The boy's father might come looking for him . . . and if he did, there was sure to be trouble.

Slowly, the wagon began to move through the rain-filled night. The horses lowered their heads against the storm. The weather had worsened and flashes of lightning illuminated the cage in which Pinocchio was a prisoner. Around the walls, the other puppets moved as the wagon passed over uneven cobbles. The room was quite dark except for an occasional brief flash of light when a street-lamp was passed . . . or lightning flashed in the mountains. The atmosphere was eerie and alarming.

Pinocchio sighed. If only he had listened to . . . he sat up excitedly. Of course — his conscience. 'Jiminy! Oh, Jiminy!' he cried excitedly. He whistled, then whistled again. 'Oh Jiminy . . . where are you?' He continued to whistle hopefully and cry out at intervals, 'Jiminy Cricket . . . Jiminy Cricket!'

The storm steadily grew worse and deafening claps of thunder rolled in from the mountains. Pinocchio was terror-stricken. This was his first experience of a thunder-storm and he pressed his hands over his ears, cowering in the corner of the cage. Presently, he began to sob. Jiminy hadn't answered his call.

Stromboli's wagon bumped along over the uneven roads and Jiminy Cricket, seated on a water pump with his umbrella raised, watched it drawing closer. Resting his chin on his hand he shook his head. 'Well, there he goes . . . sitting in the lap of luxury, the world at his feet.' He shrugged. 'Oh well, I can always say I knew him when . . .' Jiminy jumped down from the pump, landing in a puddle. The wagon drew level then passed on its slow, meandering way.

Jiminy looked sad. 'I'll just go out of his life quietly. Would like to wish him luck, though!' He stood still. 'Sure, why not?' Snapping his umbrella shut he raced off after the wagon. When he caught up with it he hopped up onto the back step, then through a gap at the bottom of the door. 'Pinocchio,' he called softly. 'Pinocchio!' Removing his top hat he shook off the raindrops. 'It's me . . . your old friend, Jiminy — 'member?'

'Jiminy!' Pinocchio could hardly believe his good luck. He started to cry. 'Gee, I'm glad to see ya!'

'Pinocchio!' Jiminy peered into the gloom. His eyes gradually became accustomed to the dimness and he moved cautiously across the floor. Then he discerned the cage just above his head and was shocked to see Pinocchio seated inside. One large hop landed him on the bars. He peered inside. 'What's happened? What did he do to you?'

Pinocchio's words fell over each other as he looked at Jiminy through his tears. 'Oh, he was so mad. He said he was going to push my face in everybody's eye!'

'Yeah?' Jiminy listened from a cross bar in the cage.

'And . . . just because I'm a gold brick . . . he's . . . he's gonna chop me into *firewood*!'

His voice was an anguished cry.

Jiminy's eyes blazed with fury. 'Oh . . . is that so! Now don't you worry, son. I'll have you outta here in no time at all!' Jiminy jumped over to the padlock to examine it. 'Why, this is just as easy as rolling offa . . . umph!' He realised it wasn't easy at all. Jiminy grunted and rattled the lock causing dust to fly in the air. Taking off his coat he hung it on a rivet and started hammering. 'Kinda rusty!' he commented. Pinocchio peered anxiously through the bars. Jiminy continued fiddling with the lock without results. 'Needs a little oil,' he remarked. Jiminy climbed right inside the lock, touching the mechanism.

He looked around and pried at the spring. Suddenly he shot out of the keyhole and whizzed past Pinocchio's nose. 'Woo! Woo!'

70

He bounced up and down, caught on a spring suspended from a bar of the cage. 'Ha, ha, ha ... must be one of the old models!' he laughed.

'You mean you can't open it?' asked Pinocchio with rising panic in his voice.

Jiminy released himself and slid down the bar of the cage. 'Yeah!' he commented dryly. Pinocchio handed Jiminy his coat and helped him on with it. Jiminy leant against the bars. 'Looks pretty hopeless. It'll take a miracle to get us outta here!'

'Gee!' All of Pinocchio's dashed hopes were expressed in that one word.

Meanwhile, kindly Geppetto, his shoulders hunched against the driving rain, a lantern swinging from his hand, stumbled along the uneven cobbles. 'Pinocchio! Pinocchio!' he cried over and over again.

A horse and wagon turned the corner and Geppetto stood aside to let it pass in the narrow lane. Stromboli had heard Geppetto's cry and was anxious to be on his way. 'Curses,' muttered the marionette master in an agitated tone. He flicked his whip across the horse's back urging it on.

If only Geppetto had known at that moment how very close his little son was . . . but he had no way of recognising Stromboli as a greedy villain, a man willing to stoop to any level to pack his money-bags with gold. Geppetto put his hand to his mouth and called again. 'Pinocc . . .' The word was drowned by a roll of thunder and carried away on the screaming wind. Stromboli's wagon disappeared over a hill, while Geppetto continued his fruitless search.

Inside the wagon, Pinocchio was sitting on the floor of his cage, Jiminy on his knee. 'A fine conscience I turned out to be,' murmured Jiminy.

A great big tear slid down Pinocchio's cheek. 'I should have listened to you, Jiminy.' He looked more dejected than ever.

'No,' said Jiminy kindly. 'It was my fault. I shouldn't have walked out on ya!'

Pinocchio sobbed harder than ever, unable to stem the flow of tears. 'I guess I'll never see my father again'.

'Aw . . . buck up, son. It could be worse!' He grinned. 'Be cheerful like me,' he quipped, then pulled a sour face. He hoped to make Pinocchio laugh — or at least, stop sobbing as if his heart would break. But Pinocchio could not stop crying. The glistening drops continued to fall down his nose and cheeks and drop into Jiminy's hat. The cricket hopped from his knee and brought a handkerchief out of his pocket. 'Aw, take it easy, son.' Leaning forward he placed the handkerchief beneath Pinocchio's nose. 'Come on — blow!'

Pinocchio blew his nose. 'Atta boy!' said Jiminy approvingly. He blew his own nose,

wiped a solitary tear from his own eye and re-
pocketed the handkerchief.

'Oh, well . . .' Jiminy glanced out of the
window. 'It's stopped raining, anyway!'

The wagon was passing along a mountain
track and as Jiminy kept his eyes fixed on the
window, he noticed a specially bright star
shining in the dark heavens. 'Hey, that star
again . . .' He sounded both nervous and
excited. 'Huh — that — lady — uh — huh —
that . . . the Fairy!'

Pinocchio fell off the swing in the cage.
Picking himself up he ran towards the locked
door, his arms extended. 'What'll she say?' He
dashed in a frantic circle round the cage.
'What'll I tell her?'

Jiminy stood against one of the bars. 'You might try telling 'er the truth!' He dived into a bird-seed cup, out of sight.

Pinocchio hid his face in his arms. He felt suddenly afraid. The light outside the window grew brighter and brighter, as the star revolved in circles. Gradually it disappeared and the Blue Fairy was revealed. She crossed immediately to Pinocchio. He had turned his back towards the door of his cage and bent over so that he peered up at the lovely lady from between his legs. 'Why, Pinocchio!' she said in a voice as sweet as honey.

Pinocchio remained in the same startling position but tried to tip his hat. 'Uh . . . ah . . . hello!'

The Blue Fairy gazed into the bird-seed cup. 'Sir Jiminy!' The cricket looked up. 'Well . . . uh . . . this *is* a pleasant surprise! Ha! Ha!' Awkwardly, feeling extremely foolish he removed his hat.

The Blue Fairy turned her large blue eyes on Pinocchio. He straightened up. 'Pinocchio . . . why didn't you go to school?'

Pinocchio hung his head, feeling ashamed. 'School? Well, I, uh . . . ' He stuck his finger in his mouth feeling tongue-tied and nervous.

Jiminy, from the bird-seed cup, prompted, 'Go ahead, tell 'er.'

Pinocchio stopped sucking his finger. 'I was going to school 'til I met somebody!'

Jiminy hopped from the inside of the cup and bowed. The fairy spoke again. 'Met somebody?'

Pinocchio nodded. 'Yeah! Uh . . . two big monsters!'

Jiminy clapped his hands to his head in an agony of disapproval. 'Monsters with green eyes . . . ' went on Pinocchio. He pointed to his own eyes. A twinkling circle of light formed on Pinocchio's nose. It increased in size then disappeared, but Pinocchio's nose had suddenly grown longer. He stared down at it in surprise . . . then felt it. 'Why . . . I . . .' he commenced.

'Monsters?' prompted the Blue Fairy.

Pinocchio batted his eyes and watched the wand in the Blue Fairy's hand. 'Weren't you afraid?' she asked.

'No ma'am . . . but they tied me in a big sack!' The twinkling circle of light made its reappearance. When it vanished, the little boy's nose was longer than ever and had begun to sprout a small tree on the very tip. Horrified, Pinocchio squinted down the extraordinary long length of his nose.

'You don't say . . .' continued Blue Fairy. 'And where was Sir Jiminy?'

Pinocchio looked at her. 'Huh? Oh . . . Jiminy?'

Jiminy hissed in Pinocchio's ear, 'Sssh . . . leave me out of this!'

Pinocchio added yet another lie. 'They put him in a little sack!'

'No!' replied the Blue Fairy. The twinkling light swiftly circled the little boy's nose yet again. This time it grew to such an alarming length that it shot right past the bars of the cage hitting Jiminy who was directly in its path. Jiminy grabbed the end of the extraordinary nose and hung onto the leaves of the newly sprouted tree.

'Yes!' said Pinocchio. He felt he couldn't back down and change his story now. When the twinkling light had vanished again, the tip of Jiminy's nose was covered with flowery bloom. Jiminy looked around in bewilderment. Where was this going to end?

'How did you escape?' asked the fairy.

'I didn't.' Warningly, the nose wiggled up and down. 'They wanted me for firewood!'

Each fresh lie made Pinocchio's nose longer and longer. The blossom on the tree grew and a bird's nest appeared amongst the foliage with tiny eggs inside. Jiminy hopped into the nest and two baby birds popped out of the fragile

pale blue shells. Jiminy looked at them in
astonishment. The Blue Fairy could certainly
work all kinds of magic.

'Oh! Oh! Look! ... my nose!' wailed
Pinocchio. 'What's happened?'

Blue Fairy looked intently at the little boy, her sweet face serious. 'Perhaps you haven't been telling the truth, Pinocchio,' she suggested.

'Perhaps!' muttered Jiminy with emphasis.

When the twinkling circle of light reappeared, flowers and leaves fell from the nest, and the birds whistled and flew away. Jiminy sat alone in the nest watching leaves falling to the ground.

Pinocchio was scared. At last he realised that the Blue Fairy could not be fooled — not even by a teeny-weeny lie and he had told incredibly big ones. His eyes filled with pleading. 'Oh . . . please help me . . . I'm awfully sorry!'

'You see, Pinocchio,' said the Blue Fairy, 'a lie keeps on growing . . . and growing . . . until it's as plain as the nose on your face.'

Jiminy hopped from the bird's nest and ran along the length of Pinocchio's nose. 'She's right, Pinoke!' He stared at Pinocchio. 'You'd better come clean,' he advised.

Looking pathetic, Pinocchio wailed, 'I'll never lie again . . . honest, I won't!'

Jiminy returned to the nest and looked up at the Blue Fairy. 'Please, your Honour . . . uh . . . I mean Miss Fairy . . . give him another chance, for my sake . . . will ya?' Jiminy crossed his hands over his chest in an appealing gesture.

The Blue Fairy nodded wisely. 'I'll forgive you this once, but remember — a boy who won't be good, might just as well be made of wood!'

'We'll be good — won't we?' Pinocchio and Jiminy both uttered the cry together then stared intently at each other. They meant to keep their word.

'Very well.' The Blue Fairy lifted her wand. 'But this is the last time I can help you.' A sparkling light sat on Pinocchio's nose and in a twinkling, it had returned to its normal length. Pinocchio rubbed his eyes for the magic lights dazzled him. Gingerly, he felt his nose. 'Gee! Look, Jiminy . . . my nose!' he cried in delight.

Jiminy danced up and down with joy. 'Hey!' he yelled. 'We're free! The Blue Fairy has set us free! Come on, Pinoke!'

The lovely fairy had vanished without trace and even though Jiminy stared into the dark, velvety night there wasn't a sign of her. Cautiously, he checked the front of the wagon.

Stromboli was sitting contentedly holding the horse's reins, his mind filled with glowing pictures of expected wealth, his eyes glued on the road ahead.

Jiminy beckoned Pinocchio and together they jumped from the back step of the wagon and dashed to the side of the road, crouching in the shadows.

Stromboli was singing is his lusty voice:

> I gotta no strings,
> But I gotta da brain,
> I buya a new suit and
> Swinga da cane . .

The sharp click of stones beneath the horse's hooves came to their ears as the wagon disappeared round a curve.

'Toodle-oo, Stromboli,' muttered Jiminy.

'Goodbye, Mr Stromboli,' echoed Pinocchio.

'Shhh!' whispered Jiminy warningly. 'Let's get out of here before something else happens.'

CHAPTER SIX

A deep hush lay over the cobbled streets of the village and a wispy fog shrouded the rustic houses. But inside the Red Lobster Inn, a disreputable tavern concealed in an alley, a cosy air of warmth embraced the smoky atmosphere. The old tap room was littered with relics of days gone by, antiques which were worth a second glance. However, Honest John and his partner in crime, Gideon the cat, were more interested in their drinks. Seated close to them on an old wooden settle was a shady character generally known by the name of Coachman. He was an unpleasant, squat man with a fat face, beady eyes and a broad nose as round and red as a ripe cherry. On his head he wore an oddly shaped hat, his coat was of dark green cloth and his black shoes were adorned with huge brass buckles.

There was something sinister about the way in which he watched his two companions through slitted eyes. The small bar parlour was wreathed in a haze of smoke, giving the room a foggy appearance. Gideon sat with his feet on the table blowing more and more smoke rings into the air.

Honest John was in good humour. His business deal with Stromboli had lined his pockets well. Lifting his pewter mug in the air, he sang:

Hi diddle dee dee
An actor's life for me,
A high silk hat and a silver cane,
A watch of gold and a diamond chain.
Hi diddle dee day
An actor's life is gay,
It's great to be a celebrity,
An actor's life for me!

Coachman stuffed his pipe with tobacco and struck a match. Tonight he had a lot on his mind. As Honest John finished his song, Giddy blew another smoke ring, caught it and dunked it into his beer, grinning foolishly. The strong brew was going to his head.

Honest John started to laugh, banged his tankard on the table and said, 'And the dummy fell for it . . . hook, line and sinker!' He chortled again as he thought of Pinocchio's innocent face.

Coachman, puffing on his pipe, drew his beetling brows together and nervously drummed his fingers on the edge of the table. He was so pleased that it had been his fortune to run into the two scoundrels. He had a proposition to make. . . but he would wait for an opportune moment. He was as sly as Honest John.

Honest John was still talking and jingling coins noisily in his pocket. 'Pinocchio still thinks we're his friends! Ha, ha, ha! And did Stromboli pay!' He dropped a heavy bag of gold onto the table. His green eyes glinted as he lit a fresh cigar. 'He paid plenty! That shows you how low Honest John will stoop! Eh! Giddy!'

He glanced across at his partner in crime, but the cat's head was immersed in his beer mug. Suddenly the feline hiccoughed and foaming liquid splashed over the table and on to his coat. He lifted his head with a slow, stupid smile.

Honest John turned to the man seated next to him. 'Now, Coachman . . . what's your

4

proposition?' The fox flicked ash from his cigar and waited.

'Well . . . how would you blokes like to make some real money?' From his bulky coat pocket the sly man took a large money-bag and flung it carelessly on the table so that the coins spilled out.

'Well,' said Honest John, his eyes immediately lighting up, 'and what do we have to do . . . eh?' He made a gesture as if slitting someone's throat.

'No, no — nothing like that, replied Coachman. 'You see,' he leaned forward, glancing round suspiciously to make sure that he wasn't overheard, 'I'm collecting stupid little boys!' His red face spread into a broad smile.

Honest John for once, was puzzled, 'Stupid little boys?'

Coachman nodded his head in affirmation. 'You know, the disobedient ones — what play 'ooky from school!'

Honest John winked knowingly. 'Ohhhhh!'

'And you see . . .' wily Coachman continued, placing his hand over his mouth, 'the boys

won't suspect . . .' He went on whispering at length while Honest John and Giddy listened. Giddy, far from sober, kept pressing his head against Honest John's ear, expecting to hear what Coachman was whispering. He caught snippets of the conversation — it sounded promising. Eventually, Coachman took his hand from his mouth and his words drifted into the smoky air. 'And I take 'em to Pleasure Island!'

Honest John and Giddy nodded approval. 'Ah, Pleasure Island,' remarked Honest John. He thought for a long moment. 'Pleasure Island?' he repeated and suddenly looked scared. 'But the law . . . suppose they . . .' Anxiously he chewed his fingernails.

Coachman waved his pipe in the air. 'No . . . no . . . there is no risk, they *never* come back . . . as boys!' He grinned evilly.

Giddy and Honest John sat close together in a frightened huddle. What Coachman was suggesting was highly illegal. If they were caught??? They didn't care to dwell on that angle, the mere thought was too devastating. Coachman laughed fiendishly and the vile sound almost curdled Giddy's blood. He ducked for protection beneath Honest John's red coat. When he peeked out again, drops of perspiration were rolling from his furry forehead. It was a risk . . . a dangerous risk. Coachman seized the lapels of Honest John's coat and looked him in the eye. He saw the hesitancy . . . but he also noticed the glint of greed. The lure of easy money always proved too much for Honest John. Coachman felt he could rely on the fox's co-operation but to add surety he banged several more money-bags on to the table. He knew he had won.

'Now,' he said, 'here's where you come in.' The three conspirators put their heads together. 'I've got a coachload leaving at midnight tomorrow. We'll meet at the crossroads . . . and no double crossin'.'

Coachman's voice was a threat.

Even Honest John didn't relish the idea of crossing Coachman. 'No sir!' he replied with conviction.

Coachman used his finger on the table to outline a certain district of the village. 'Scout around . . and any good prospects you find, bring 'em to me.'

'Yes, Chief.' Honest John was feeling easier already; his conscience seldom bothered him for more than a few seconds at a time.

Coachman said in a stage whisper, 'I'll pay you well . . . I've got plenty of gold.'

'Yes, yes, yes!' Honest John was now very eager. The three scoundrels downed their drinks and stealthily departed from the Red Lobster Inn. Soon they had merged into the mist.

When Pinocchio and Jiminy made their escape from Stromboli's wagon, the village where Geppetto lived was a long way off. Pinocchio was very sleepy after the events of the evening and Jiminy suggested seeking shelter for the night. Eventually, they had found a barn where a number of young calves were resting in sweet-smelling hay. Pinocchio and Jiminy had crept in and curled up in the warm atmosphere and were soon sleeping like tops. Directly dawn flooded in a blaze of apricot glory across the eastern skies, Jiminy had woken Pinocchio and they had moved on. By the following night, the two weary travellers reached the outskirts of the village where Geppetto lived. Jiminy felt a great sense of relief to see the outline of the quaint houses through a wispy mist. At last he would be able to take Pinocchio safely home . . . and how overjoyed the toy-maker would be.

Pinocchio trod firmly on the cobbles, a determined look on his face. 'No sir, nothing can stop me now. I'll make good *this* time!'

Jimmy hopped ahead. 'You'd better,' he

flung over his shoulder.

'I will . . . I'm going to school!'

'That's the stuff, Pinoke.' Jiminy opened his umbrella and used it as a parachute to sail along above the pavements. It was easier than hopping all the time.

Pinocchio murmured thoughtfully, 'I'd rather be smart than be an actor!'

'Now you're talking!' agreed the cricket. 'Come on, slowpoke — I'll race ya' home!'

Jiminy hopped onto the wall of a small bridge they were crossing and Pinocchio started to race across it. When they reached the other side, Jiminy was in the lead, determined to be first. He would wait for Pinocchio on Geppetto's porch. Pinocchio ran as fast as his little legs would carry him though he was no match for Jiminy's giant hops. It was just as he was dashing past a shadowy alley that a cane seemed to come from nowhere and hook itself

round his arm. He tried to run on, then struggle free ... but he was trapped.

'Well, well, Pinocchio ... what's your rush?' The smooth voice of Honest John assailed Pinocchio's ears.

'I gotta beat Jiminy home.' Hastily, the little fellow tipped his hat, saying as an afterthought, 'Oh, hello!'

Honest John stepped from the shadows. 'Well, how's the great actor?'

'I don't want to be an actor.' Pinocchio pointed up at the fox's face saying seriously, 'Stromboli was terrible!'

Honest John's face assumed an expression of sympathy. 'He was?'

'Yeah ... he locked me in a birdcage!'

'He did?'

Giddy grinned behind Pinocchio's back and polished his fingernails on his bright yellow tie. Pinocchio said firmly, 'Uh huh ... but I learned my lesson ... I'm going ...'

Honest John interrupted. 'Oh, you poor, poor boy! You must be a nervous wreck!' He clapped his hands to his head. 'That's it! You *are* a nervous wreck!' Placing his fingers on Pinocchio's nose he frowned, then shook his head. From his inside pocket he brought out reading glasses and slipped them on. 'We must diagnose this case at once.' With an air of authority he cleared his throat. 'Quick, Doctor ... your notebook!' Giddy walked out into the open, a pencil and notebook in his hand.

Honest John held Pinocchio's wrist as he pretended to take his pulse. 'Bless my soul!' he mused aloud. 'Hmmmmm ... ummmmm ...'

Pinocchio looked at his wrist — it looked perfectly normal to him. Honest John was shaking his head. Studying his watch, he commented, 'My, my! Just as I thought ... a slight touch of monetary complications ...' Hastily, Giddy began to write in his notebook. 'Yes,' went on Honest John, his expression grim, 'with bucolic semi-lumar contraptions of the flying trapezius.' The fox held back Pinocchio's head and peered down his throat. 'Um . . . say hippopotamus!'

'Hi-ho-ha-ha-uh . . .' Pinocchio stumbled over the strange word.

'I knew it,' said Honest John with conviction. 'Giddy, make sure you take all this down. Compound transmission of the pandemonium with percussion of spasmodic frantic disintegration!' When Giddy's writing pad was full, he dotted his letters in the air. Pinocchio looked very troubled, now. He didn't understand what all this was about.

Honest John placed his spectacles on the end of Pinocchio's nose. 'Close your eyes,' he ordered. The little boy did as he was told. 'What do you see?' asked the fox.

Pinocchio shook his head. 'Nothing!'

Swiftly, the artful fox placed a spotted handkerchief in front of the glasses. 'Open your eyes . . . now what do you see?'

'Spots!'

Honest John whisked the hanky away. 'Ah hah!' Bending down, he lifted Pinocchio's shirt and placed his ear close to the boy's chest. 'Now the heart . . . Oh!' He started back in pretended dismay. 'Palpitating syncopation of the killer diller, with a wicky wacky stomping of the floy joy! Get this, Giddy . . .' The cat wrote on the back of his notebook and danced in rhythm to heartbeats.

Honest John's diagnosis was at last complete. 'Quick, Doctor, that report!' The fox snatched the book, hastily perused the scribbled notes and said, 'This makes it perfectly clear!' He tapped the notebook ominously. 'My boy, you are allergic!'

Pinocchio, balancing awkwardly on one leg, looked distressed. His clothes were dishevelled and he felt suddenly sick. 'Allergic?' he asked.

'Yes! And there's only one cure!' Honest John looked directly into the boy's face. 'A vacation! Yes — on Pleasure Island.' Giddy, in the background, snickered.

'Pleasure Island?' questioned Pinocchio, his voice full of wonder.

Honest John and Giddy joined hands and circled round the bewildered Pinocchio, singing and dancing. 'Yes . . . that happy land of carefree boys, where every day's a holiday!'

'But I can't go . . . I . . .'

The fox chuckled and slapped Pinocchio on the back. 'Why, of course you can go!' He slid his arm around the boy's waist in a pretended gesture of friendship. 'I'm giving you *my* ticket! Here!' He handed Pinocchio a playing card — the ace of spades.

Pinocchio held the card at arm's length. 'Thanks, but I'm . . .'

'Aw . . . tut, tut, tut . . . but I insist . . . your health comes first!'

Giddy sneaked up behind Pinocchio, his trusty mallet held almost over the boy's head. Honest John motioned him to put it away. 'Come,' he said in his most cordial tones, 'the coach leaves at midnight.' Giddy and Honest John each took one of Pinocchio's arms and swiftly marched their little victim in the direction of the crossroads where they were due to meet Coachman.

Honest John, well pleased with his night's work, sang as they walked over the cobbles:

Hi diddle dee dee
It's Pleasure Isle for me
Where every day's a holiday
And kids have nothing to do but play.

Confused and unable to wriggle free, Pinocchio was led along between the villains.

Jiminy Cricket arrived at Geppetto's home and waited in the stone porch for Pinocchio. He kept peering along the street. What was keeping Pinocchio? He hopped around with impatience, then decided to go back and look for him. Perhaps he had fallen over and was hurt. Rounding a corner, Jiminy was astonished to see Pinocchio firmly in the grasp of Honest John, and Giddy. 'Pinoke!' he yelled loudly, cold fear clutching at him. 'Oh, Pinoke! Now wherever is he?'

The words of Honest John's song fell on his ears. 'Huh!' muttered Jiminy, sure now that his impending sense of disaster was correct.

The trio turned into an archway, the words of the song still lingering in the air. 'Hi diddle dee dee — it's Pleasure Isle for me . . .'

Jiminy hopped over to the archway, his heart in his boots. 'Pinocchio! Hey, come back . . . come back . . .' The trio didn't hear his cries; even if they had, Honest John would not have freed his victim. Pinocchio again represented the promise of wealth to the greedy fox. From the crossroads, the impatient whinnying of horses filled the night. They were anxious to start their long journey. The village clock struck the hour of midnight and each successive stroke filled the air with dark foreboding.

CHAPTER SEVEN

Everything happened so quickly that Pinocchio was aboard the coach almost before he realised what was happening. The inside of the vehicle was already packed with noisy little boys, laughing and joking. Each one of them was excited, anticipating the delights of Pleasure Island. There wasn't room for Pinocchio so he found himself seated out in front with Coachman and another boy. Still feeling bewildered, he tried to stifle his sense of fear. Everyone else was so happy that he tried to brush aside his feelings of being trapped like a fly in a spider's web.

Coachman was beaming broadly, his black eyes almost hidden by his fat cheeks. He had hoped for a full coachload . . . but the quota

had more than exceeded his wishes. He could afford to be jocular. He flicked his whip lightly over the backs of the animals and the coach rumbled off into the gloom.

Honest John and Gideon had already disappeared, covetously carrying their ill-gotten gains. The country road was long and winding and the outlines of the trees slid by like grey, melancholy ghosts. Pinocchio sighed as he remembered Jiminy. He hoped the cricket wouldn't be angry because Honest John had convinced the little boy that he needed a vacation. The complaints had sounded very serious. Odd though, he didn't feel ill — just a little sick inside at leaving the village behind before he had seen dear Geppetto again.

Pinocchio felt a sharp nudge and looked round into the face of the boy seated next to him. In the swaying light from the coach he could make out a freckle-faced, ginger-haired boy. He wore a funny grey hat with a yellow feather stuck at a jaunty angle. The boy grinned, showing a row of protruding teeth. The night air was chilly and he pulled his blue woollen muffler close to his throat. Pinocchio smiled shyly as Coachman cracked his whip and yelled 'Giddyup.' The mules broke into a fast trot. There was a lot of mileage to cover before daylight and Coachman had no intention of being late. It would have been a source of comfort to Pinocchio if he had been aware that at that very moment, Jiminy Cricket was seated, albeit a trifle uncomfortably, at the rear of the coach. He had attached his open umbrella to a metal ring and was sitting inside it. Every now and again he sneezed violently as clouds of dust rose from the wheels and went up his nose. 'Well,' said Jiminy, resting his chin on his hand with an air of resignation, 'here we go again!'

The boy sitting next to Pinocchio said suddenly, 'M'name's Lampwick, what's yours?' Taking a slingshot from his lap he took careful aim at a tree trunk.

Pinocchio politely tipped his hat before replying, 'Pinocchio!'

Lampwick nodded. 'Ever been to Pleasure Island?' he asked, shooting again but this time at a hedge.

Pinocchio shook his head and pointed to his card — the ace of spades. 'Uh-uh. But Mr. Honest John gave me . . .'

'Me needer . . .' cut in Lampwick, obviously overjoyed at the prospect of a visit, 'but day say it's a swell joint . . . no school . . . no cops . . . you can tear da joint apart and nobody says a woid!'

In the murky light, Coachman grinned as he listened to the conversation. Everything was going according to plan. He loved contented fools. Flicking his whip like a long, thin snake he urged the mules to even greater speed.

'Honest John gave me . . .' Pinocchio started again.

Lampwick wasn't listening. His head was full of fantastic dreams. 'Loaf around . . . plenty to eat . . . plenty to drink . . . yeah! And it's all free!' He licked his lips.

'Honest John . . .' No matter how hard poor Pinocchio tried, he could not command Lampwick's attention.

Lampwick knocked against Pinocchio, pushing his hat over one eye. 'Boy — dat's da place. I kin hardly wait!' Jumping to his feet on the swaying coach he used his slingshot to hit a white fence.

Several hours passed and at last the first streaks of a pearly dawn pierced the dark sky. The mules thundered down the country lanes at a steady gallop. A hump-backed bridge caused all the boys to yell joyously as the coach bumped over it. Sensing that the first part of their journey was almost over, they screamed their delight as the first rays of the sun lit the hedgerows.

The coach entered a long, dark tunnel.

When it emerged, there was a splendid vista of blue sea, rose-splashed sky and flying, swooping gulls. A shiny white boat bobbed up and down in the tiny harbour. Stage one of the journey was complete. With deafening shouts of enthusiasm the boys flung themselves on board, anxious to be on their way to Pleasure Island. Pinocchio, jammed in the crush, was practically hurled onto the small craft but soon got caught up in the infectious air of enthusiasm surrounding him on all sides. Coachman smirked, mentally patting himself on the back.

The journey to Pleasure Island was a short one, but for the impatient boys it could not be over soon enough. As the boat docked, a drawbridge dropped into place. The children shouted 'hurrah' and scrambled wildly from the boat, eyes gleaming.

Pleasure Island was all they had wished for — and more! They swarmed up the beach towards a carnival. A barker, dressed in red and blue clothing waved his arms in welcome, crying in a loud voice, 'Hurry, hurry, hurry, hurry . . . right here, boys, right here . . . get your cake, pie, dill pickles and ice cream . . . eat all you can . . . be a glutton . . . stuff yourselves . . . it's all free, boys. It's all free . . . hurry, hurry, hurry, hurry!'

The excited boys needed no second bidding. They fell over each other in the scuffle to be first. The air was full of gaily coloured balloons as some of the more rugged boys charged towards a tent labelled 'Rough House'.

The barker in charge yelled, 'The rough house . . . the rough house . . . it's the roughest, toughest joint ya' ever seen. Come in and pick a fight, boys!' A scene like bedlam developed as boys of all shapes and sizes took up the challenge.

Lampwick rounded a corner, close to the 'rough house' tent. He was munching a leg of chicken; clutched in his other hand was a

large dill pickle. 'Oh, boy, a scrap!' he said
enthusiastically. He turned to Pinocchio who
was licking an ice-cream cone while trying to
balance a piece of lemon meringue pie in his

left hand. 'Let's go in and poke somebody on da' nose!'

'Why?' asked Pinocchio standing close to the tent's entrance.

'Aw . . just for the fun of it!'

'OK Lampy.' Pinocchio tossed his ice-cream and pie over a hedge. The two boys puffed out their chests and strutted inside. Soon they were kicking, punching and shrieking with the rest of the boys.

Jiminy Cricket had endured the dusty, uncomfortable journey on the rear of the coach, and at the last minute had managed to hop aboard the boat to the island. His intention of catching up with Pinocchio directly they landed, had badly misfired. They boys' headlong rush to gratify their various desires had left Jiminy gasping. They had charged ashore like a pack of wild horses and the cricket was lucky that thudding feet had not trampled him into the sand.

Jiminy wandered around Pleasure Island observing the numerous side-shows, the mountains of food, the pool tables, gambling tents, drinking saloons, stacks of cigarettes and cigars, and an over-abundance of temptations which would make a good boy, bad — and a bad boy, abominable. The more he saw, the more worried he became. Something was wrong . . . very wrong. No adult would indulge the whims of boys to such an extent unless there was something evil, really sinister behind it. Jiminy had a hunch that before long, trouble would be brewing in more ways than one.

Tipping his hat to the back of his head, he watched carved wooden Indians automatically throwing fat cigars to eager boys. A grinning barker yelled above the din, 'Tobacco Road . . . Tobacco Road. Get your cigars, cigarettes and chewin' tobacco. Come in and smoke your heads off. There's nobody here to stop you . . . help yourselves, boys!' The words renewed Jiminy's fears. 'Pinocchio,' he murmured, 'oh,

Pinocchio. There's something phoney about all this. I've gotta get him out of here!'

Regardless of personal danger, the cricket hopped in and out amongst dozens of feet as he tried to locate his little charge . . . but without success. Further distractions for wilful boys added to Jiminy's premonition of danger. Almost in disbelief, he surveyed a model home. The notice on its exterior, read: 'Model Home — Open For Destruction!' Already a bonfire blazed in the front garden as a group of zealous boys, thirsting for fresh adventure, tore into the furnished rooms of the house. The barker encouraged their acts of devastation. Furnishings were pulled on to the lawn as further fuel for the fire; a piano was rolled down a flight of stairs; stones were flung through windows and pots of paint daubed over newly decorated walls. Bricks were hammered, and slates knocked off the roof. Jiminy, hiding behind a boulder, shuddered in horror as a barker nodded approval. 'It's all yours, boys, it's all yours. Do your worst!' Within a short time the building was in a state of collapse, practically razed to the ground.

Pinocchio and Lampwick were inside the house, but they had entered by a back door so Jiminy had not seen them. Lampwick, a cigar in his hand, strutted across to an oil painting covered with childish scribbles. He struck his match on the picture's surface. 'What'd I tell ya? Ain't dis a swell joint?' He smiled, showing his protruding teeth.

'Yeah! Being bad's a lot of fun, aint it!' Pinocchio, despite earlier doubts, was enjoying himself.

Lampwick picked up a brick. 'Yeah . . . uh huh!' He pointed across the room. 'Get a load of that stained glass window!' He flung the brick as hard as he could. It was a direct hit; glass shattered into a hundred fragments and he clapped his hands. This was really living.

On a bridge, close to the carnival entrance,

stood Coachman cracking his long, snake-like whip. He was shouting orders to a bunch of rough-looking characters who were working for him. 'All right, now . . . 'op to it, you blokes! Come on, come on, shut the doors and lock 'em tight!'

The men nodded. 'Now git below and git them crates ready!' Coachman's grin was evil, as hands on hips, he looked towards the carnival. 'Hmmm . . . give a bad boy enough rope and he'll soon make a jackass of himself!' He roared with fiendish laughter as though at some private joke. The kids had been having a good time but now the tables were about to be turned.

Jiminy did not give up his search for Pinocchio, though with each passing minute, he grew more anxious. Chaos, debris and signs of wholesale destruction surrounded him on all sides. Apart from having fallen into the ways of very naughty boys, he could also be in considerable danger. 'Pinocchio . . . Pinocchio . . .' called Jiminy again and again. The worried little cricket wandered amongst the ruins, looking disconsolate. 'Where is everybody?' he asked of no one in particular. Suddenly, the place was like a graveyard. Jiminy shook his head. 'I don't like the looks of this! Pinocchio . . . Pinocchio . . . where are you?' His voice carried away on the breeze. There wasn't an answer . . . only the fierce crackling of the bonfire as it blazed brightly, illuminating the desolate scene. Jiminy sighed. He wouldn't give up — he must look further.

Pinocchio and Lampwick had found their way into a pool hall. Apart from themselves it was quite deserted . . . which if they had stopped to consider it, seemed rather odd. Pinocchio, comfortably seated in a chair, with his legs propped on a table, had a cigar in his hand. A mug of beer and a pile of coins lay on a table beside him. He looked casually around the hall. 'Where do you suppose the kids went to, Lampwick?'

Lampwick wasn't interested. Standing in a cocky pose at the pool table, he spat on the floor and flicked ash from the end of his cigar. 'Aw, they're around somewheres . . .' Lining up his cue he took a cross side shot. 'Whatta you care . . . you're havin' a good time, ain't cha?' Lampwick jumped onto the edge of the table to take a back hand shot. He rather fancied himself as a pool player.

'Uh huh . . . I sure am having a good time,' agreed Pinocchio.

Lampwick's shot was successful and he chalked on his cue tip with the burning cigar. 'Oh boy! Dis is da life . . . huh, Pinoke?'

Pinocchio leaned back, stretching luxuriously. 'Yeah! It sure is!' He puffed on his cigar, blowing wreaths of smoke into the air.

'Aw . . . you smoke like me grandmudder!' remarked Lampwick with a snicker. He hit the cue ball and flipped his cigar in the air, catching it again. 'Come on . . . take a *big* drag — like dis!'

Pinocchio blinked as he watched his friend. 'OK Lampy!' He drew on the cigar, inhaling deeply. Within seconds his face turned a vivid red. Hastily, he removed the cigar from his mouth . . . smoke rings popped out of each ear. His eyes began to water and then he turned a sickly shade of green. As he exhaled, an enormous smoke ring floated up towards the ceiling.

'Huh — some fun, eh, kid?' Lampwick giggled.

Pinocchio, looking peculiar and very pale managed to say weakly, 'Yes . . . oh yes!'

Lampwick reckoned up his score. 'OK Slats . . .' He turned to Pinocchio. 'Your shot.'

Still feeling nauseated, Pinocchio climbed shakily on to the pool table, the cigar clenched between his teeth. Taking the cue, he raised himself to his knees. As he looked at the eight ball it seemed to move. Suddenly he grabbed his throat . . . he felt horribly sick. But he wasn't yet ready to give in. He tried to line up a shot again though his eyes boggled and he couldn't focus clearly.

'What's da matter, Slats?' shouted Lampwick above the smoky haze. 'Losing your grip?'

It was at that precise moment that Jiminy Cricket squeezed under the swinging doors of the pool room. The sound of voices had drifted to his ears as he was passing . . . there was always the faint hope that Pinocchio might be around. The cricket looked up in startled dismay when he spied Pinocchio leaning on the pool table ready to play.

'Pinocchio . . . Pinocchio . . .' yelled Jiminy angrily. So stunned was the little boy at hearing the voice of his conscience, dear Jiminy, that he completely fluffed the shot, ripping the green baize cloth. Then he fell flat on his face.

'So . . . this is where I find you!' Jiminy hopped onto the table surveying the torn felt and a dazed, sickly looking Pinocchio.

Pinocchio's cigar was squashed flat, grey ash clung to his mouth and for some reason, when he gazed at Jiminy, the cricket looked oddly distorted. 'How do you ever expect to be a *real* boy?' asked Jiminy in disgust. He hopped across the table 'Look at yourself!' Reaching over, he flung the cigar onto the floor. 'Smoking! Playing pool!' He kicked the eight ball hard, then rubbed his toe. 'Oww!' he spluttered, 'that hurt!' He turned his attention back to Pinocchio. 'You're coming right home with me . . . this minute!'

Lampwick stepped forward, a frown on his freckled face. He scooped Jiminy off the table, holding him up to his eyes. 'Hey!' he asked Pinocchio, 'who's da beetle?'

Jiminy swung angrily at Lampwick with his umbrella. 'Let go . . .' he yelled indignantly. 'Put me down!' Lampwick suspended Jiminy by his coat-tails, grinning broadly. Jiminy spun helplessly in the air, then became enmeshed with his coat and his umbrella. 'Let me get out of here . . . let me out of this!' His angry tones were muffled by his coat.

Pinocchio knelt on the pool table. He was both stunned and confused by Jiminy's unexpected appearance. Suddenly, everything seemed complicated and too bewildering to sort out. 'He's my conscience,' he said in a small voice to Lampwick. 'He tells me what's right and wrong!'

'What?' Lampwick looked aghast and dropped Jiminy hastily onto the pool table. 'D'you mean to tell me you take orders from a grasshopper?' His tone implied that he certainly would not do such a thing.

Jiminy, now recovered from the shock of his ordeal, adjusted his hat and glared. 'Grasshopper!' he shouted, jumping to his feet. 'Look here . . . you . . . you . . . impudent young pup, it wouldn't hurt you to take orders from your grasshop . . . er . . . er . . . your conscience.' Removing his hat, he shook his finger in Lampwick's face and jumped on to the eight ball. 'That's if you have one!'

Lampwick picked up his cue to make another shot. 'Yeah, yeah . . . yeah . . . sure!' he shouted at Jiminy and hit the cue ball. The shot was accurate and it struck the eight ball sending Jiminy rocketing across the table, trying deperately to maintain his balance. 'Screwball in the corner pocket,' laughed Lampwick maliciously. Jiminy let out a loud yell as he rolled into the trough, landing with a bump on his bottom. His hat fell off. Another ball bounced into the trough and it was only Jiminy's presence of mind that saved him from being hit on the head. Swiftly, he ducked to one side, muttering, 'Woo . . . woo!' Lampwick was a dangerous menace.

Jiminy dragged himself over the edge of the pocket, his clothes sadly dishevelled. Lampwick's coarse laughter assailed his ears. Though very small, Jiminy stood his ground.

'Why you . . . ya young hoodlum . . . I'll . . . I'll knock your block off!' Discarding his coat, he tossed his umbrella aside and adopted a fighting pose from his position on the table. 'Why . . . I'll take ya apart . . . and out cha back together!'

Pinocchio, still sitting on the edge of the pool table, made a move at last. He reached over and grabbed Jiminy by the vest. 'Oh,' he pleaded, 'Don't hurt him, Jiminy . . . he's my best friend!'

Jiminy swung round, stung by Pinocchio's remark. 'Your best friend? And what am I?' He pointed to himself. *Just your conscience!* He picked up his coat and hat. 'OK. That settles it!'

An expression of doubt crossed Pinocchio's face. 'But Jiminy . . .'

Jiminy, very angry and hurt, put on his coat back to front without even noticing. 'You buttered your bread . . . now sleep in it!' Provoked and furious, he stomped along the edge of the pool table and as he wasn't looking where he was going, he fell into a corner pocket, then yelled as he slid down the chute and onto the floor. It was a long drop. He fell in the midst of a heap of cigar butts, much to Lampwick's amusement.

Jiminy clambered to his feet with as much dignity as he could muster. 'Heh, heh, heh. Go on . . . laugh . . . make a jackass outta yourself!' Waving his hand wildly in the air, he glared at Pinocchio. 'I'm through! This is the end!' Turning on his heel, he made for the exit.

'But, Jiminy . . .' called Pinocchio plaintively, 'Lampwick says a guy only lives once!'

Jiminy glanced over his shoulder. 'Lampwick! Huh!'

Lampwick was filling two mugs with beer. Grinning, he called to Pinocchio, 'Come on . . . come on . . . let 'im go!'

CHAPTER EIGHT

Jiminy made his departure from the pool room in a great fury. Apart from being very angry, he was also bitterly disappointed in Pinocchio. Lampwick would continue to influence the boy and lead him into bad ways . . . but there seemed little that Jiminy could do. Pinocchio would not listen! Jiminy muttered under his breath as he hopped along. 'Lampwick! Huh! Lampwick! That burns me up! After all I tried to do for him. Who's his conscience, anyway? Me . . . or that hoodlum, Lampwick?'

Hopping up a flight of stairs, he said, 'I've had enough of this! I'm taking the next boat outta' here!' He turned in the direction of the harbour. The boat was being loaded with crates so Jiminy stole aboard and pounded on a door. 'Open up . . . open up! I wanna go home!' No one came in answer to his knocking, but he could hear the braying of donkeys. Jiminy listened in astonishment. Donkeys? What was going on?

An unpleasant but familiar voice sounded above the plaintive animals. Coachman yelled, 'Come on, you blokes, keep 'em movin'!' Rough looking men in shabby clothes hustled to and fro, unloading droves of donkeys from chutes and pushing them onto the boat. 'Lively there now — we haven't got all night!' shouted Coachman in a voice of authority.

Jiminy, crouching out of sight, watched the baffling scene. 'Where'd all the donkeys come from?' he asked himself. It was a mystery. He hadn't noticed any of them when he was wandering over Pleasure Island.

Yet another donkey was pushed off a chute and flung on board. 'Come on . . . come on . . . let's have another!' Coachman stood with hands on hips, watching every move with beady eyes.

A donkey, wearing clothes and a hat, slid down the chute and stopped opposite Coachman. 'And what's your name?' asked the unpleasant man. The animal brayed loudly and Coachman nodded his head in satisfaction, tearing off the donkey's clothes. 'Okay, you'll do — in you go!' He kicked the creature and laughed. 'You boys'll bring a nice price . . . ha, ha, ha . . . all right, next!' Another donkey pushed forward was wearing a sailor suit and looked very sad. Its ears drooped. Coachman grinned and leaned over. 'And what might your name be?'

'Alexander!' replied the donkey.

'Ummmmm! So you can talk!'

'Yee . . . yes sir!' The donkey started to sob pathetically. 'I wanna go home to my mama!'

Coachman pushed the donkey aside. 'Take 'im back,' he yelled to one of the men, '. . . 'e can still talk.'

Alexander, sobbing bitterly, crashed into a wall. As he got to his feet he cried, 'Please! Please! I don't wanna be a donkey . . . let me outta here!'

Coachman's eyes blazed with fury and his snake-like whip cracked through the air. Donkeys waiting on the quay-side raised their ears in fright and cowered down. 'Quiet!' yelled Coachman. 'You boys have had your fun — now pay for it!'

Jiminy Cricket blinked his eyes in horror. 'Boys!' he said. 'Oh, my goodness!' He clapped his hand to his head in a gesture of despair. 'So

that's it . . . Pinocchio . . . oh, Pinocchio!'
Despite Pinocchio's naughtiness, Jiminy could
not desert him. He would have to endeavour to
get him off the island somehow. Knowing the
terrible fate that awaited the disobedient boy,
he hopped ashore and across the carnival
grounds . . . back to the pool room.

Lampwick was still playing pool. A mug of
beer stood at his elbow and a lighted cigar
burned a hole in the edge of the table.
'Huh . . .' he commented, taking a side shot,
'to hear dat beetle talk, you'd tink sompin' was
gonna happen to us!' At that exact moment,
Lampwick's normal ears disappeared and a
pair of donkey's ears sprouted in their stead.
Pinocchio, sprawled in a chair drinking beer,
thought his eyes must be playing tricks.
Hastily, he banged the beer mug down on the
table.

Yeah . . .' continued Lampwick. 'Conscience! Aw . . . phooey!' He moved around the
table; a long tail suddenly shot out of the seat
of his trousers. Pinocchio threw away his cigar,
convinced he was having hallucinations.

As yet, Lampwick was unaware of what was
happening to him. He took another shot.
'Where he git dat stuff? How do you ever
expect to be a real boy?' He straightened up.
'What's he tink I look like . . . a jackass?'
Turning, he faced his friend.

Pinocchio couldn't restrain himself — he
burst out laughing. 'You sure do!' he giggled.
Lampwick had grown a donkey's head.
Lampwick *did* look funny. But all of a sudden,
Pinocchio clapped his hand over his own mouth
. . . his laugh had turned into a donkey's bray.

'Hey,' said Lampwick jeeringly, 'you laugh
like a donkey.' As he spoke, his voice turned
into a bray. 'Did that come outta me?' he asked
with a frown.

Frightened now, Pinocchio nodded 'Yes.'

Gingerly, Lampwick felt his face and chin.
Alarm filled his voice 'Oooooooh!' He felt his

cheeks — then his ears. 'Hey, what the . . . what's goin' on?' Dashing to a full length mirror he surveyed his image. With a scream, he turned to Pinocchio. 'Aw . . . I've been double-crossed!'

Pinocchio, appalled at what was happening, stuck his finger in his mouth. He was terribly frightened. What could he do?

Lampwick ran frantically up and down the length of the pool room. 'Help! Help! Somebody, help! I've been framed! Help!' Crawling on his knees he moved towards Pinocchio. 'Please, ya gotta help me, Pinoke! Be a pal . . . call da beetle . . . call anybody!' Lampwick's hands changed into donkey's hooves right beneath Pinocchio's nose. He backed away, his face aghast. 'Oh . . . Maa . . . maaa!' brayed Lampwick. 'Mama! Mamaaaaa!!' He dropped down on all fours, a complete donkey. Kicking and braying in fear, he galloped to the mirror on the opposite wall and smashed it into tiny fragments.

Pinocchio opened his mouth but no words came out. Fear had temporarily taken away his speech. Lampwick continued on his rampage of destruction. Bucking furiously, he upset the table, chairs, playing cards and beer. Confusion became chaos. The last loose remnants of his torn clothes fell to the ground, a pathetic pile of rags. Lampwick was a donkey in every aspect.

Pinocchio closed his eyes and ducked as a chair landed beside him. Something felt very odd on his head. Cautiously, he touched his ears, then cried out in dismay. Horror of horrors . . . he was turning into a donkey, too. 'Oh, what's happened!' he wailed. 'Oh . . . oh . . . what'll I do?' His eyes boggled as a donkey tail shot through the seat of his pants.

Jiminy approached the pool room in a breathless rush. 'Hope I'm not too late.' He slid beneath the door. 'Pinocchio!' he cried.

'Jiminy . . . Jiminy . . . help!' Pinocchio

turned beseechingly towards his true friend.

'Quick . . . Pinoke . . . the kids . . . the boys . . . they're all donkeys!' gasped Jiminy. His eyes widened when he looked at Pinocchio properly. 'Ooooh! You too! Come on . . . quick . . . before you get any worse!'

Pinocchio and Jiminy dashed from the pool room as fast as they could. 'This way, Pinoke! It's the only way out!'

Pinocchio climbed a wall and scrambled over a pile of rugged rock, Jiminy grimly hanging on to his tail. 'Hurry up,' urged the cricket, 'before they see us.'

Eventually they reached a part of the shoreline that lay some distance from the harbour. Faintly, in the distance, they could hear the braying of donkeys. 'Ya gotta jump,' yelled Jiminy.

Pinocchio took a flying leap from a cliff and fell into the sea with a great splash. Down . . .

down . . . down . . . went Pinocchio before he managed to surface. Desperately, he clawed for the rocks to support him. Finally, wet and exhausted, he struggled ashore with a very bedraggled, half-drowned Jiminy still clinging to his tail.

'Jiminy . . . uh . . . Jiminy! Are ya . . . you all right?' The cricket slid off Pinocchio's tail and sat on the ground. 'Sure!' he said wryly, patting his cheek so that he squirted water like a fountain. He coughed. 'For a moment there, I though we'd never make it. It certainly feels good to be back on dry land!' He lifted up his hat and a shower of water doused him. Nodding sagely he murmured, 'Come on — let's get home!'

It wasn't an easy journey back to the village. Pinocchio and Jiminy were forced to wait till darkness clothed Pleasure Island. Then they rowed back to the mainland in a tiny dinghy. Once ashore, they were fortunate in seeing a wagon bound for their village. The old farmer, seated contentedly up front talking to his horse, didn't know that he was carrying two extra passengers snuggled well down in the fragrant load of hay he was transporting. When the familiar cobbled streets came into view, Pinocchio and Jiminy jumped off the wagon and hurried along the street towards the toymaker's cottage. Pinocchio called out as he ran, 'Father . . . Father . . . I'm home!' Dashing into the old stone porch he tried the latch but the front door wouldn't open. Standing on tiptoe, he pulled the bell and knocked loudly on the door. 'It's me, Pinocchio! I'm home to stay!'

'Home again!' said Jiminy with evident relief. There had been times when he'd wondered if they would ever make it. Using his umbrella, he pounded on the door, too. 'Here he is, Mr Geppetto. Home at last!' Jiminy twirled his umbrella like a drum major's baton while the two of them waited on the doorstep. Minutes ticked by . . . not a sound came from inside the house. 'Maybe he's asleep,' suggested Jiminy. From the ledge of the porch, he hopped onto a window sill.

'Father! Father!' Pinocchio called impatiently. 'It's me.'

Using his handkerchief, Jiminy rubbed a clean spot on the dusty window pane and peered inside. What he saw gave him an uneasy feeling. Geppetto's bed was neatly made up but the room had a dusty uncared-for look; the workbench was covered with cobwebs and Figaro's little basket was empty. 'Pinoke . . . come here!' Pinocchio also peered through the window. 'Look!' whispered Jiminy. 'He ain't here!'

'He . . . he's gone!' Pinocchio's voice trailed off sadly.

'Yeah . . . and Figaro and Cleo, too,' said Jiminy. Even Cleo's fish bowl had a fine cobweb spun over its surface. The quaint room had a pathetic, dejected air.

Pinocchio and Jiminy went back to the stone porch and sat down together, looking extremely miserable. This was an unexpected calamity. 'Maybe something awful happened to him,' said Pinocchio mournfully.

Jiminy tried to console him, despite niggling doubts and fears. 'Don't worry, son! He probably hasn't gone far.' They sat in silence, each busy with their thoughts, each of them worried. Long minutes passed. Gradually, the sky turned green, rose and gold in the west, the sun sank beyond the horizon and a few faint stars began to twinkle. Birds twittered noisily as they returned to their nests and secret resting places. Pinocchio felt lonelier than ever without Geppetto. He sunk his head in his hands.

Overhead, a snowy white dove suddenly appeared, carrying a newspaper in her mouth. She let it go and it drifted slowly down, right on to the porch where Jiminy and Pinocchio were

huddled together. Jiminy was the first to notice the paper. 'Hey,' he said jumping to his feet. 'What's this?' Putting on his spectacles he peered at the newsprint. 'It's a message.'

'What's it say?' asked Pinocchio curiously.

Jiminy pointed at the writing with the tip of his umbrella. 'It's about your father!'

'Where is he?' The boy's voice brightened instantly.

Jiminy dropped the paper and it fluttered to the ground. 'Why . . . uh . . . it says here . . . uh . . . he went lookin' for you, and uh . . . he was swallowed by a whale!'

Pinocchio dropped to his knees to stare at the newspaper. 'Swallowed by a whale?' he asked, full of despair.

'Yeah! A whale. A whale named Monstro!'

'Oh . . . he's . . .' Pinocchio's voice was an agonised wail.

'But wait! He's alive . . .' went on Jiminy.

'Alive? Where?'

111

Jiminy hopped across the columns. 'Why . . . uh . . . inside the whale . . . at the . . . bottom of the sea!'

'Bottom of the sea?' repeated Pinocchio in incredulous tones. After a moment's thought he straightened up and stuck out his chin. As Jiminy pocketed his glasses, Pinocchio walked off up the street.

'Hey! Where you going?' called Jiminy.

'I'm goin' to find him!' Pinocchio's voice carried a wealth of determination.

Jiminy raced after him. 'But, Pinoke . . . are you crazy? Don't you realise he's in a whale?'

'I've gotta go to him!' insisted Pinocchio, hurrying on.

'Hey! Pinoke! Wait! Listen here, son.' Jiminy's pleas for common sense were in vain. Pinocchio wanted nothing as much as to see dear Geppetto again. He was willing to take a risk . . . any risk to enable his dearest wish to come true.

So Pinocchio and Jiminy set off on yet another journey . . . this time to the ocean where it was generally known that Monstro, the enormous terror of the seas, had his home. By the following morning they had reached the cliffs overlooking the water. Green, snowy crested waves dashed themselves against the rocky shoreline and misty clouds of spray flew into the cool air.

Pinocchio ran to the cliff edge and studied the rocks. Selecting one which suited his purpose he tied his donkey tail to it, making the knot secure. Jiminy stood watching. 'But this Monstro . . . I've heard of him and he's a whale of a whale . . . why . . . he swallows whole ships alive!' Jiminy was anxious for Pinocchio's safety, but his little friend was not influenced by his words at all. 'Tie the knot good and tight, now,' advised the cricket. 'And besides, it's dangerous . . . why . . . uh . . .'

Pinocchio got to his feet and faced Jiminy. Extending his hand he said, 'Goodbye, Jiminy!'

'Goodbye?' Jiminy couldn't conceal his surprise. 'Oh, no. I may be live bait down there in the ocean, but I'm with you!' He stood ready to take the leap with Pinocchio.

Pinocchio smiled and grasped his rock, for he needed its weight to carry him into the ocean

depths. Jiminy stood ready, his umbrella clasped in one hand and holding his nose with the other. 'Right,' he said. 'Come on . . . let's go!' As they sailed through the air, he cried 'Look out below!'

As Pinocchio hit the water, he let go of the boulder. Tied to his tail, it dragged him down . . . down . . . down beneath the surface, into a new and wonderful world. The green water, suffused with golden light from the sun, gradually deepened to emerald, then to a dark bottle-green. Different varieties of fish, startled by the sight of the little boy, swam rapidly in the opposite direction. 'Gangway, down there!' Jiminy called out.

At last they reached the sea bed. Pinocchio sat down on the sand. 'Gee! What a big place!' he exclaimed, looking round. Luxurious meadows surrounded them; fields of waving grass, brightly coloured flowers, a variety of bushes and a wealth of plants. Scattered over the sand were shells of assorted shapes, some with frilly edges, others shaped like spindles and harps. Some of the shells were musical and played a tune as water flowed through them. All the while, tall reeds whispered mysteriously.

Jiminy was having a problem staying beneath the water and his hat kept floating upwards. Finally, he anchored himself to a rock by using his umbrella. He patted it affectionately . . . he wouldn't be without it, for it was always useful.

When Pinocchio was rested he got to his feet. 'Come on, Jiminy,' he said.

'All right! Soon as I take on some ballast!' A fish swam towards Jiminy, staring directly into his face. 'One side, sister!' Jiminy pushed the impudent fish out of his way and picking up a handful of small rocks, placed them inside his hat. Very gingerly, he placed the hat on his head. He didn't want a headache. The added weight should keep him from rising towards the surface. He staggered beneath the weight of the load. 'So long,' he murmured to a nearby fish,

began to walk away and turned suddently up-
side down. He was top heavy.

A fish, very curious at Jiminy's strange
antics, turned onto its back to stare. 'Hmm,'
said Jiminy. 'Put the ballast in the wrong end.'
He would have to drop the rocks inside his
trousers. He started to do so and spied a fish
peeking at him through a clump of reeds.
'Humph!' he muttered in disgust. 'No more
privacy than a goldfish!' The rocks were cold
and he shivered. 'Ooohh . . . chilly!'

Pinocchio was already some distance ahead.
As he walked slowly through the waters, he
called in a loud voice, 'Fatherrrr! Fatherrrr!' In
the strange atmosphere, the sound was weird
and mysterious. Even the plants thought so;
they shrunk back, until they practically disappeared. Great clam shells snapped shut, but
when Pinocchio moved away, they opened
again. But not for long. Jiminy cried out, 'Hey,
Pinoke . . . wait for me!' The clams closed . . .
clearly they did not welcome strangers.

'Father!' repeated Pinocchio.

'Father!' called Jiminy. 'Huh,' he said
suddenly. 'He ain't *my* father.' Cupping his
hand to his mouth, he yelled, 'Mr Geppet-
tooooo!' A fish following Jiminy made a sudden
lunge and grabbed his umbrella, knocking the
cricket to the ocean floor. Jiminy snatched his
umbrella back. 'Turn loose . . . let go . . . run
along . . . you . . . you little squirt!' The fish, a
baby one, opened its mouth and within a few
seconds, its furious-looking mother arrived on
the scene. She glared at Jiminy in menacing
fashion, gliding towards him. Discretion was
the better part of valour. Jiminy backed away.
'What's the matter?' he gulped. 'Can't a fellow
. . . I was only . . .' In his anxiety to escape, he
tripped over a rock. 'We were only looking for
Monstro,' he tried to explain. At the mention
of the dreaded whale, both mother and baby
fish shuddered in horror and flashed rapidly
out of sight.

Jiminy looked after their shadowy forms and blinked, almost in disbelief. 'That got 'em!' he mused to himself.

As Pinocchio made his way through the reeds, a variety of fish and strange shell-like creatures followed him. The rock, still tied to his tail, was cumbersome but he plodded on, dragging it after him. Surely someone must know where Monstro was hiding, and help him find his father. A small, friendly fish darted up the sleeve of his jacket. Pinocchio giggled, saying, 'Oh, hello!' to it. The fish swam across his back and down the other sleeve. 'Oh. Uh, can you tell me where to find Monstro, the whale?' The little fish stiffened in fear and zipped away. All the other fish followed, leaving Pinocchio alone and dazed. 'Gee! They're really scared!'

Jiminy had decided to try a little investigation on his own. Politely, he knocked on the door of an oyster shell, using his umbrella. The shell opened a fraction. Jiminy tipped his hat. 'Uh . . . pardon me, pearl . . . are you acquainted with Monstro, the whale?' Without so much as a reply, the oyster clammed shut and immediately bored its way deep into the sand. Seconds later, bubbles drifted upwards.

'Whoa . . . hold it there,' shouted Jiminy as he got caught up inside one bubble, his hat in another. Reaching out with his umbrella, he hooked his hat, bursting the bubble. 'Huh!' he muttered as he swam on. He wasn't receiving any co-operation . . . none at all.

Pinocchio continued pushing his way through the lush underwater growth. Already, barnacles were clinging to his rock and a multitude of other tiny creatures. Jiminy finally caught up with him and pulled a starfish away. 'One side there, son!' Hopping on to the boulder, the cricket yelled, 'Come on, boys . . . break it up . . . break it up there!' He sat down, determined to keep off all newcomers. Sea horses danced in pursuit, lively and curious.

'Hey, what tha . . . whoa, whoa, whoa, quit shovin' now!' The sea horses swarmed round, eager to investigate these strangers in their midst. 'Whoa . . . don't crowd there . . . take it easy . . . take it easy, there!'

Pinocchio glanced at the new arrivals and grinned with delight. Their saucy, captivating ways made him laugh and he temporarily forgot his problem. One of the horses, cheekier than the rest, jumped onto his finger and then onto the tip of his nose.

'Whoa . . . whoa . . . whoa there, whoa!' Jiminy was riding on the back of a sea donkey. It was pleasant, the easy rhythm much better than being dragged and bumped through the reeds on Pinocchio's boulder. 'Steady, there, Nellie,' whispered Jiminy in his steed's ear. 'Go ahead, Pinoke . . . ask them!'

Pinocchio made an appeal to the sea horses. 'Could any of you tell me where to find Monstro?' The effect of his words were devastating. The friendly sea horses exchanged anguished looks with one another, then darted out of sight. Not a trace of them was to be seen. Even the sea donkey that Jiminy was riding bucked furiously. Jiminy's pleas were in vain. 'Whoa . . . whoa . . . boy!' he cried, gradually sliding off into the reeds; the donkey vanished with the speed of lightning.

'Fatherrrr . . . . . father!' Pinocchio's voice trailed into the distance.

'Mr Geppettoooooo!' shouted Jiminy.

The reeds rustled and whispered mysteriously, echoing their cries . . . a musical shell sang a song . . . but Mr Geppetto did not reply.

CHAPTER NINE

Some distance away, on the bottom of the sea bed, Monstro the whale lay asleep. He was snoring loudly, causing water around his massive head to eddy and ripple. The surrounding area was deserted, as shoals of fish sought to avoid close contact with Monstro at all times. But though he dozed, there was

activity in the enormous cavern inside him.

Through a faint, wispy mist which led to his giant stomach, Geppetto and Figaro were sitting on the rail of their boat. Geppetto had a fishing pole and Figaro lowered his tail into the water, each of them hopeful that a fish would

take their bait. They had been waiting for a long time and Geppetto sighed. 'Not a bite in days,' he said.

Figaro's mournful expression was also reflected in Cleo's face. She swam around looking miserable and considerably thinner than usual. With very little optimism, she dived under the rocks of her goldfish bowl, searching diligently just in case there was a morsel of food she had missed. There wasn't!

Geppetto shook his head sadly. 'We can't hold out much longer!' He sneezed. 'Achooo! Achooo!' It must have been catching, for Figaro sneezed too. The violence of his sneeze almost knocked him off the boat-rail.

'I never though it would end this way, Figaro.' The pretty black and white cat dejectedly rubbed his nose with his paw. 'Imagine starving to death in the belly of a whale,' continued Geppetto.

Figaro padded over to his beloved master and snuggled against him with a display of love and affection. Geppetto stroked his shiny fur and tickled his ears. 'My poor little Pinocchio,' continued the toy-maker sadly. 'He was such a good boy!' Raising his fishing pole, he examined it. 'Empty!' he said. His sigh echoed through the cavern. 'It's hopeless, Figaro.' Figaro meouwed in sympathy. 'There isn't a fish left,' said Geppetto. 'If the monster doesn't soon wake up . . . I . . . I'm afraid we are done for.'

Monstro the whale stirred in his sleep. He had been dreaming of a delicious meal . . . hundreds of fresh, silvery fish. The dream was so real that it awakened his appetite. Yes, he *was* hungry. Warily, he opened one eye. A school of fish were swimming towards him. Swiftly, he dropped the shutter over his eye like a blind, pretending to be asleep. The fish almost collided with him, then, shocked at the close proximity of their dreaded enemy, slipped away into the shadows. But they were not quite fast enough. Monstro opened his mouth and twirled in the water. Like a tidal wave, water and fish were carried inward, powerless to resist.

Way down inside the whale's cavernous stomach, Geppetto's boat rocked violently. 'Here they come!' he called. 'Tuna . . . it's tuna.'

Fish flooded into the whale's stomach, leaping in confusion. Geppetto ran along the boat deck. 'Food! We will eat!' He cast his line with immediate success. 'Here's a big one,' he yelled joyously, tossing it over his shoulder. The huge fish landed on the edge of a fish bin, and a startled Figaro jumped, then knocked it aside.

Now that Monstro was awake, he decided to hunt for an entire shoal of fish. He had overslept and felt very empty. The tuna were only a light snack. Pinocchio was seated on a ledge wondering what he should do next, when hundreds of fishes rocketed past him. He blinked in amazement, wondering where they were off to in such a hurry.

'Hey,' he called. 'Wait a minute, have you seen . . .'

The mighty whale swam powerfully through the waters, crashing, splashing and causing a great commotion. Terror-stricken fish dashed frenziedly in all directions. Pinocchio spied a great grey shadow approaching. After one swift glimpse he had no doubts about the creature's identity. He leapt up, startled out of his wits. 'Monstro . . . it's Monstro,' he yelled in panic.

Jiminy jumped onto Pinocchio's back, clapping his hand to his head in fright. 'Woo . . . we gotta get outta here!'

But with the rapid surging of the waters, Pinocchio's tail had become wedged beneath his boulder. Distraught, he thrashed and tugged and pulled in an effort to free himself. It was no good. He was trapped! Quick-thinking Jiminy rapidly ran down the length of

Pinocchio's tail and unwound the knot. Pinocchio broke loose and shot forward at devastating speed. Jiminy just managed to grasp the end of his tail in time. Fear lent wings, and Pinocchio cleaved through the water at such a high burst of speed that he outdistanced the fish.

'Woo hoo hoo . . . come on, Pinoke! Don't wait for me!' urged the cricket who had managed to make his way up to Pinocchio's nose. He slid off and continued swimming close to his friend.

Meanwhile, deep down inside Monstro, there was a terrific hive of activity. Geppetto braced himself against the ship's rail. 'Never saw so many,' he yelled as the little craft rocked violently with the buffeting of the fish. A giant wave crashed over Geppetto, submerging him and washing over the decks. Fish shot in all directions.

'Whoops!' Geppetto managed to maintain his balance. 'Hah, hah, hah. Here's another one . . .

Figaro clung to the side of the fish bin during the deluge, pushing the fish inside when they grew too lively and threatened to jump out.

'Enough for weeks,' yelled Geppetto gleefully. 'Ah . . . here's a big one!' It flipped into the bin, hitting Figaro on the chin. The little cat peered over the edge and fell right inside, landing on a fish's back. It thrashed wildly, slapping Figaro with its tail. He leapt smartly back onto the deck and put up his fists, ready for a fight. He wasn't going to have those big fish bullying him.

Geppetto called over his shoulder, 'Keep them in there, Figaro!'

A huge fish tail flashed in the air and caught Figaro square on the face, knocking him sideways. Groggily, he sank to the deck and shook his head. Inside Monstro, it was either feast or famine.

Pinocchio had been caught up in a giant

shoal of fish all trying to escape, but Monstro
was rapidly gaining on them. Pinocchio peeked
over his shoulder. The whale was too close for
comfort, and yet . . . if he was to ever find dear
Geppetto . . . he must go inside the monster.
Bravely, he scrambled over the backs of fleeing
fish towards Monstro's mouth. The fish rushed

upwards . . . the whale followed. They all broke
the surface of the water . . . the fish . . .
Pinocchio . . . and the whale. The fish and the
boy were spouted upwards like a fountain. The
fountain descended . . . the whale's mouth was
waiting . . . it snapped shut!'

Overhead, gulls screamed and curved and wheeled in flight. The crashing waters calmed and within a little while, the surface was as smooth as glass. Monstro, the fish and Pinocchio had all vanished into the gloomy depths. But the whale surfaced again. Now that he had trapped the fish, the giant whale lay passively on the water, his enormous appetite appeased.

But Jiminy Cricket had not been caught. His trusty umbrella had opened out, carrying him high into the air. Now he descended at a leisurely pace, the umbrella acting as a parachute. As Jiminy floated down, he passed the whale's open eye and saw himself reflected as clearly as though in a mirror. Gently, he landed on the water, inside the umbrella.

'Hey!' said Jiminy boldly. 'Hey blubber-mouth, open up . . . I gotta get in there!' Jiminy leaned forward and pounded on the whale with his fist.

Meanwhile Geppetto, deep inside the whale, continued fishing from his boat. He was making sure of a plentiful supply of food this time. 'Looks like the last of them,' he grunted to Figaro, casting his line again. 'Here's a big one . . . only a few left. We gotta work fast!' Feeling yet another bite, he reeled in the line and a fish sailed right overhead, landing directly in the bin. Pinocchio, clinging to that particular fish's tail, also flew through the air. He floundered amongst the fish, holding out his arms and trying to scramble back to the deck. Eventually, he managed to get to his feet, though standing on dozens of lively fish in a bin was a slippery business.

'Here's another one,' called Geppetto excitedly, for he had not yet noticed Pinocchio.

'Hey, Father!' Pinocchio yelled. 'Father!'

Geppetto turned from the boat rail and waved. 'Don't bother me now, Pinocchio,' he answered absent-mindedly. The toy-maker cast his line once more then suddenly, with a startled cry of realisation, he leapt towards the boy. Pinocchio extended his arms in welcome. At last ... at long last ....

'Father!' He wobbled uncertainly on the slippery, floundering fish. As Geppetto attempted to snatch him to his bosom, Pinocchio was slapped down by a huge tail and sank into the bin.

Geppetto, his eyes closed, overcome by emotion, didn't notice. 'Pinocchio, my son!' Fondly he kissed his son ... at least for a brief moment he imagined it was his beloved son ... in actuality, it was a fish.

'Hey Father, here I am!' Pinocchio pushed a small fish from the top of his head. Comprehension dawned, and Geppetto quickly dropped the fish he was holding. 'Huh ... huh ... oh ... oh ...' Pinocchio leapt through the air, landing in Geppetto's arms. 'Yes, yes. Oh Pinocchio! My boy, my dear boy! Ha, ha ... I ... I ... am so very happy to see you!'

'Me, too, Father!'

Figaro, not wanting to be left out of the family reunion, jumped onto Geppetto's head. 'Whoops!' Geppetto laughed as Figaro slid down on his chest, forcing himself between Geppetto and Pinocchio.

'Figaro ... aw, Figaro.' Pinocchio's voice was filled with happiness as he petted the little cat, who snuggled contentedly under his chin, purring loudly.

Cleo, watching from her bowl, bounced excitedly up and down, trying to attract attention to herself.

'Cleo ... oh Cleo!' Tears of joy shone in Pinocchio's eyes. 'You're here, too!' For all of them it was a wonderful, wonderful moment.

Geppetto carried his son and his cat over to Cleo's bowl. Fondly, Pinocchio petted the pretty goldfish and Figaro slid down onto the deck.

'Yes ... we're all together again,' said Geppetto, happily embracing Pinocchio. He could hardly believe it. Pinocchio sneezed. 'Oh, you're soaking wet!'

'Yes, Father!'

Geppetto set him down on a barrel. 'You . . . you mustn't catch cold!' he said in concern.

'But I have come to save you!'

Geppetto smiled sadly, as he moved over to his bed to remove the quilt. The gravity of their situation was once more uppermost in his mind. Figaro was standing on the quilt and as it was pulled away, he meouwed his protests and slid on to the deck.

'You . . . you . . . shouldn't have come down here!' said Geppetto, wrapping Pinocchio lovingly in the warm quilt.

'But Father . . .'

'Though I am awfully glad to see you! Heh, heh . . . let me take your hat.' Reaching over, he removed his son's hat. His eyes widened in horror and he clapped his hand to his head, looking aghast. Pinocchio's donkey ears had popped into view.

'Ohhhhh!' stammered Geppetto.

Figaro and Cleo stared in fright, then Figaro took refuge behind Cleo's bowl. She hid in her castle, peeping out in amazement.

'Pinocchio!' Geppetto sounded puzzled.

'Wha . . . what's the matter?'

Geppetto stuck his fingers in the air. 'Those ears!'

'Huh! Ears!' nodded Pinocchio. He blinked and tried to pull his ears down to make them look shorter. His quilt fell off. 'Oh, these! Huh . . . ha . . . oh . . . that's nothing, I got a tail, too!' Reaching for it, he twirled it and laughed . . . a donkey laugh. He clapped his hand over his mouth in concern. It did sound very odd.

Figaro, now perched on the brim of Cleo's bowl, hopped back in alarm . . . and fell right in. He surfaced with an excited miaow, shaking himself. He hated getting wet. Pinocchio, standing on the barrel, looked ashamed and very sheepish. 'Pinocchio,' asked Geppetto.

'What's happened to you?'

'Well ... I ... I ...' He twirled his tail again and hung his head.

Geppetto managed a smile. 'Oh, oh, never mind now ... old Geppetto has his little wooden-head ...' He sighed. 'Nothing else matters!' He embraced the little boy then with a display of affection, they rubbed noses, laughing together.

Monstro was basking on the surface of the water. He felt comfortably full and relaxed. Overhead, the seagulls dived, squawked and quarrelled over scraps. Jiminy was still endeavouring to get inside the whale. He knew Pinocchio was down there somewhere in that cavernous inside, and probably Geppetto, too. But how to join them ... that was a major problem. Monstro was not at all co-operative. Jiminy pounded on the whale's teeth, using his umbrella. 'I gotta get in ... my pal's in there! Come on, ya big moose ... open up, I tell ya!'

Monstro ignored Jiminy completely ... but the seagulls did not. They nose-dived, pecking at him with their sharp beaks. 'Hey! Cut it out!' Jiminy sailed through the air and landed on a bottle. Hastily, he climbed inside. It was a temporary refuge from the seagulls, who were determined to pester him. 'Hey! Beat it ... beat it, ya buzzards!' Thankful for his ever useful umbrella, he thrust it through the neck of the bottle and floated around Monstro.

While Jiminy was trying to figure how he could get *in*, Geppetto, Figaro and Pinocchio were wondering how they could ever get *out*. Geppetto was not over-optimistic about their chances. The trio were seated on the boat-deck, talking the matter over. 'Get out ... oh no, no, son. I've tried every way ... why ... I ... I've even built a raft!' He pointed to the water below.

'A raft?' questioned Pinocchio. 'Why ... that's it!'

'Huh?' Geppetto looked puzzled.

Pinocchio jumped to his feet. 'We'll take the raft . . . and when the whale opens his mouth . . .'

Geppetto gestured. 'No, no, no, no! Now listen, son, he only opens his mouth when he's eating. Then everything comes in, nothing ever goes out!' He sniffed pessimistically.

'Oh!' Pinocchio looked miserable and twirled his tail in his hand. His idea had at first seemed a good one . . . but his father knew best.

Geppetto got up and took Pinocchio's hand. 'It's hopeless, Pinocchio. Don't think about it. We'll make a nice fire and cook some of this fish!'

Pinocchio stood stock still, jerking his hand free. 'A fire! That's it!'

'Yes . . . and then we'll all eat again!'

But Pinocchio wasn't listening. His mind at that moment was not registered on food . . . but escape. 'A great big fire! Lots of smoke! Quick . . . some wood!'

Geppetto and Figaro could not follow the little boy's flow of thought. 'Smoke?' said Geppetto. 'Oh yes, sure . . . smoked fish will taste good!'

Pinocchio had already disappeared. He returned with a chair and smashed it over a barrel. 'Pinocchio, not the chair!' said Geppetto reprovingly.

Pinocchio paid no heed to his father's words. 'Hurry, Father . . . more wood.' His voice was a crescendo of rising excitement.

Geppetto was vexed. 'Oh, what'll we sit on if . . . if . . .'

Pinocchio picked up a lantern. 'We won't need it. We're getting out.' He threw the lantern on to the wood-pile and it immediately caught fire, igniting the wood.

Geppetto and Figaro exchanged bewildered looks. 'Getting out?' asked Geppetto. 'But how?'

Pinocchio picked up the quilt which had

been wrapped round him and flung it amongst the flames. 'We'll make him sneeze!'

'Make him sneeze? Ohhh!' Realisation dawned on Geppetto. It was a brilliant idea. His little wooden-head was smarter than he had thought. 'That will make him mad,' warned Geppetto, thinking of the danger. Even as he spoke, great billowing clouds of smoke began to rise, forming ominous, murky shadows.

CHAPTER TEN

On the surface of the water, all looked calm. Monstro was sleeping, while gulls rested on his back. He was dreaming of gliding through tropical waters. That was hardly surprising for the bonfire raging deep in his inside was making him feel very warm. The thought of escape — actual freedom after days of being cooped up inside a dark cavern — had fired Geppetto and Figaro to enthusiastic efforts. The whale opened his mouth and roared. Smoke belched forth.

Jiminy, paddling around in his bottle, said, 'Well, it's about time!' He managed to paddle past the whale's giant teeth. At last he was inside.

Down below, Pinocchio and Geppetto were pushing their raft towards the whale's mouth. Figaro and Cleo were sitting on it, looking hopeful. Geppetto had doubts. 'It won't work,' he said. 'Hurry, Father! Climb aboard!' ordered Pinocchio.

'We'll never get by those teeth,' said the toymaker glumly.

'Yes, we will!' Pinocchio reached up and pulled down the sail, tying it round the mast.

Jiminy, about to paddle downstream to the whale's interior, was astonished to see Pinocchio and Geppetto approaching the exit. 'Hey! which way you goin' . . . wait for me!'

Jiminy paddled furiously with his umbrella.

Geppetto and Pinocchio jumped aboard the raft at the last minute and Pinocchio shouted gleefully, 'Hang on . . . here we go!' The whale, smoke pouring from him in clouds, prepared to sneeze.

When it finally came, the sneeze was a mighty one. The raft spun round and round at rapid speed, then with everyone clinging on grimly, it was washed out past the whale's teeth and onto the surface of the ocean. At the same time, Jiminy floated out on his bottle. 'Gesundheit!' he called, racing past the whale in a flurry of spray. But though they were outside Monstro, they were certainly not out of danger. The whale was inhaling deeply for another sneeze. His giant breath was sucking the raft back inside. It was a terrifying ordeal. 'We're going back!' shouted Geppetto frenziedly.

'No! We'll make it . . . faster . . . faster' repeated Pinocchio. They paddled furiously until their arms ached with fatigue. The wash sucked them closer and closer. 'It's no use . . . we're done for,' said Geppetto gloomily. The whale sneezed again. The little raft zoomed and spun as though caught in a giant whirlpool, bouncing, then subsiding into deep water troughs. Gulls screeched and flew in circles close to their heads, threatening to knock Figaro and Cleo into the sea. The combined efforts of Geppetto and Pinocchio carried them into calmer waters.

Pinocchio raised his paddle jubilantly. 'We made it!'

Monstro had not yet inhaled enough water to put out the fire below . . . and he was in a foul temper. Ducking his head he bellowed. Geppetto pointed. 'Look, now he *is* mad!' The whale rose in the air then charged through the waters like a mad bull, causing giant waves. Geppetto and Pinocchio started paddling desperately again. 'I told you he would be furious!' called Geppetto above the spume.

The whale dived deep into the churning. waters. 'Ah . . . he's gone!' said Geppetto, his voice full of relief.

Pinocchio stopped paddling. His arms ached. 'Where'd he go?'

Before there was time for a reply, the raft rose high in the air and the whale swished past. 'Look out . . . there he is . . . hang on!' cried Geppetto.

The powerful tail caught the edge of the raft, tipping it up. Geppetto, Pinocchio, Cleo and Figaro were flung into the sea. It was a bad moment. Pinocchio was the first to clamber back onto the raft, and he helped the others aboard. His breath came in deep gasps. 'He's coming back . . . oh please, hurry!'.

'He's trying to kill us, son!' Geppetto and the boy resumed paddling. 'Wow . . . here he comes again!'

Monstro was rushing through the water, leaping in the air, diving . . . surfacing . . . and all the time he kept the raft in his sights. As Geppetto had observed, the whale was out for a kill, but neither Pinocchio nor Geppetto were ready to give up.

'Look out!' cried Geppetto in alarm. 'Jump!'

No other line of action was possible. Together, they dived beneath the surface as their raft smashed into smithereens. Monstro had done his work and he looked with satisfaction at the pieces of debris floating on the sea's surface.

Seconds later, Pinocchio bobbed up from the depths. 'Father! Father!' he called in distress. Where was he? Surely all their combined efforts had not been in vain? He cried out again. 'Father!'

Geppetto was clinging to a log. 'Pinocchio,' he cried weakly, 'swim for the shore.'

The whale surfaced some distance away. 'Hang on, Father!' called Pinocchio.

'Save yourself,' whispered Geppetto, close to drowning. The log floated away and Geppetto slipped down into the waters. They closed over his head. Pinocchio dived, and after a struggle, managed to raise Geppetto to the surface. The waters were churning again. He glanced over his shoulder in fright. The whale was still dangerously close.

Towing Geppetto, Pinocchio struck out bravely for shore. A rocky coast lay some distance away . . . if he could only last out!

Geppetto had now lost consciousness and was a dead-weight, but Pinocchio struggled bravely on with his burden. The rocky shore still seemed a long way off, and he felt very, very tired. Monstro had not given up after all. He continued to charge through the water coming closer and closer. A wave, fiercer than the rest, carried Pinocchio forward. The next moment he felt the jagged rocks beneath his feet. The whale flung himself towards them, his mouth open, but he was too late. He couldn't go closer for fear of being stranded. Sea gulls pecked his back, then scattered with raucous cries.

Well nigh exhausted, Pinocchio towed Geppetto towards a large cave, helped and hindered in turn by the waves which swept over the rocks and swirled all around him. At last, Pinocchio dragged his father inside the depths of the cave. He sank down, unable to drag himself another step. The wind howled and the waves crashed and suddenly the cave's interior was a swirling mass of water. Geppetto, still unconscious, was caught in the backwash and sucked out onto the cruel rocks. The next wave carried him further inland to a stretch of sandy beach.

Only a few yards from where Geppetto lay in a pathetic, sodden heap, Figaro was scrambling ashore towing Cleo, still intact in her goldfish bowl. How the two of them had survived was a miracle . . . but there they were! Figaro's once-beautiful silky coat clung to him, as, drenched and miserable, he shook himself vigorously.

When he had gained sufficient strength, he padded across the sands to where Geppetto lay. The toy-maker was in a bad way, his breath coming in short, hard gasps. His eyes were closed but he muttered over and over,

'Pinocchio . . . save yourself . . . save yourself.'
Figaro lovingly licked his master's cheek.
'Don't mind me, son, save yourself . . .
Pinocchio . . .' The old man's voice trailed off
into silence. Figaro looked sadly at Geppetto,
and snuggled close to his cold, wet body,
meowing piteously. A solitary tear trickled
down his furry cheek.

Not too far away, Jiminy Cricket was
standing on his bottle. It had been washed up
onto the beach with his umbrella and lay on
the sands beside him. Hopping down, Jiminy
squelched across the beach towards the rocks.
His instinct told him that it was there he would
find Pinocchio. He called out, 'Pinocchio . . .
Pinocchio . . .' The roguish wind and ruthless
waves carried his voice back to him.
Clambering over the sharp rocks, he looked
around. Then he spotted the brave boy and
Jiminy's voice became a lament. 'Oh . . .
Pinocchio . . . Pinocchio,' he groaned. The
brave little fellow was lying face down in the
surf as it washed viciously amongst the rocks.
There wasn't a sign of life.

Some hours later, Geppetto recovered sufficiently to drag himself across the beach and gather his little family round him. But when he saw that Pinocchio, his dear little Pinocchio was dead, he wept bitterly. It was only due to his brave efforts that Geppetto and the others were still alive. The boy's clever scheme to escape from Monstro had been successful . . . for everyone but himself. Broken-hearted, he carried Pinocchio home to the village.

At the house, the toy-maker laid brave Pinocchio on the bed and knelt down beside him weeping bitterly. 'My boy . . . my dear little boy!' His frame shook with sobs as he bent over the inert form. Figaro was crying unashamedly and Cleo looked very miserable and lay on the bottom of her bowl with a dejected air. As for Jiminy Cricket, he too, was inconsolable. He sat close to a candle burning in a holder, wiping his streaming eyes with his handkerchief. He couldn't believe that his dear little Pinocchio would never speak to him again.

Suddenly, Jiminy noticed something that the others did not. Through the open window floated a bright light which grew even brighter and formed a twinkling circle. From its centre stepped the Blue Fairy, love and compassion on her beautiful face.

Softly, she whispered in Pinocchio's ear, 'Prove yourself brave, truthful and unselfish, and some day you will be a *real* boy!' Her wand flashed in her hand. 'Awake, Pinocchio, awake!'

Gradually, the twinkling light faded, then vanished altogether. At that moment, Pinocchio made a faint movement. His eyes opened and, miracle of miracles, he was transformed into a *real boy!* Instantly, he sat up, rubbed his eyes and looked around him with a startled expression. He stared at Geppetto crying beside the bed. 'Father!' he

asked, leaning forward and touching him.
'Whatchà crying for?'

'Because you are dead, Pinocchio!'

Pinocchio shook his head vigorously. 'No . . .
no, I'm not!'

'Yes . . . yes you are!' Despairingly,
Geppetto waved his hand in the air. 'Now lie
down.'

'But, Father,' insisted Pinocchio, 'I'm alive,
see, and . . . and I'm . . . I'm . . .' His voice rose
in excitement. 'I'm a *real* boy!' Jiminy, from his
position on the candle holder, looked at
Pinocchio with true joy. The Blue Fairy had
kept her word!

Geppetto raised his head at last. 'You're alive?' His voice was filled with wonder. How could this be? Reaching over, Geppetto picked Pinocchio up, holding him close. Yes, it really was true. He could scarcely believe it. 'You're

alive and . . . and . . . you *are* a real boy!' His happiness knew no bounds.

Jiminy threw his hat in the air, followed by his umbrella. 'Whee! Whoopee!' he yelled as loudly as he could.

Geppetto's tears had turned to laughter, hysterical laughter. It was indeed a miracle. 'Hah, ha, ha . . . a real live boy!' He whirled the delighted Pinocchio round and round.

Figaro, completely overwhelmed by the unexpected and wonderful event, grabbed Cleo and kissed her. The little fish blinked her eyes in amazement, then fluttered her eyelashes. Pinocchio was alive and Figaro loved her. It was a wonderful world.

Geppetto danced all around the room, hugging Pinocchio and looking as if he would never tear his eyes away from the smiling face he loved so well. 'Hah, hah . . . this calls for a celebration!' He struck all the clocks into life — the clocks that had been silent for so long. The pendulums started swinging, the mama

clock resumed spanking her naughty child, the hunter clock struck the hour, and Figaro jumped up setting in motion the clocks which Geppetto had missed. The room vibrated with life and heartfelt happiness.

Geppetto wound up the music-boxes too. 'Professor . . . lots of music,' was his command to the leader of the band on top of one of the boxes. Delighted as a child, he ran round the room winding up one box after another until the air was a sweet cacophony of sound. The bear's music-box and the elephant's box too tinkled merrily.

Geppetto placed Pinocchio on the floor, and taking his hands, whirled him round the room. Picking up his accordion he struck a few harmonious chords, then started to play a merry jig. Figaro danced in front of Cleo's bowl; she swam and swayed her fan-tail in rhythm to the music. A spontaneous air of gaiety pervaded the atmosphere of Geppetto's quaint and wonderful workshop. After many trials and tribulations, the true joy of living was ready to open up for little Pinocchio.

Jiminy put on his hat and picked up his umbrella. He looked at the happy scene, murmuring, 'Well, ahah, this is practically where I came in!' Glancing towards the window he looked out at the blue velvety sky. One star shone brighter than the others. He hopped on to the window-sill and stared hard at it. It was a wonderful night. A soft, fragrant breeze breathed on the village and in the distance, the snow-covered mountains shimmered in the silvery light from a crescent moon.

Looking skyward, Jiminy said in a soft voice, 'Thank you, Milady, he deserved to be a real boy!' He paused. 'And it sure was nice of you to . . .' The bright star became brighter. Jiminy, startled, scratched his head. 'Huh? Why . . . wha . . . wha . . .' He looked down at the lapel of his coat. 'Well, I'll be . . .' A badge glittered in the evening light. It said: *Official Conscience — 18 ct.*

'Ho, ho, ho, my . . . my . . .' Jiminy was so
overwhelmed that for a moment he couldn't
speak. Proudly, he rubbed the badge with his
lapel. 'Solid gold, too!' he finally managed to
comment. He flashed it in the moonlight. 'Oh,
I think it's swell!' He gazed from his perch on
the window-sill out over the sleepy, quaint
village where he had first met Pinocchio on a
night that seemed so very long ago. He still
thought it was a very beautiful village, with its
cobbled streets, its ancient steeple, and the
gold weather-vane that accurately forecast all
weather. His heart was full. 'Thank you, Blue
Fairy,' he whispered, then started to sing:

When your heart is in your dream,
No request is too extreme,
When you wish upon a star,
Your dreams come true!

NOW FOR THE FIRST TIME

Walt Disney

SUPER 8MM HOME MOVIES

OFFER THE **FUN** OF BOTH

DISNEYLAND & DISNEY WORLD

IN YOUR OWN HOME

SPECIAL OFFER FOR NEW ENGLISH LIBRARY READERS

✱A DAY AT DISNEYLAND
Here's a cherished souvenir that lets you relive the excitement
and charm of Disneyland right in your own home! Enjoy a thrilling
Matterhorn descent, Mickey Mouse and other favourite Disney
characters, The World of Tomorrow, the fascinating Haunted
Mansion, Bear Country and the delightful It's A Small World...
a joyous film journey that shows why Disneyland is called
"The Happiest Place on Earth."

**✱VACATION WONDERLAND AT
WALT DISNEY WORLD**
All the fun doesn't take place inside the Theme Parks—there's a
world of family sport and amusement at the Vacation Wonderlands.
Relive happy memories of the recreational facilities every time
you show these films. Enjoy again the Polynesian Village, Monorail,
rides, Fort Wilderness camp-grounds, fireworks and water-ski
shows...and much, much more!

**YOURS
FOR ONLY
£6.15** incl.
VAT
SAVE 40%
ON NORMAL
RETAIL PRICES

ALL YOU DO

© WALT DISNEY PRODUCTIONS

SEND CHEQUE/P.O. + 15p POSTAGE and PACKING MADE
PAYABLE TO WALT DISNEY PRODUCTIONS LTD. TO:
WALT DISNEY PRODUCTIONS LTD., 83 PALL MALL LONDON S.W.1.

PLEASE RUSH ME:
A DAY AT DISNEYLAND ....COPIES
VACATION WONDERLAND AT WALT DISNEY WORLD...........COPIES

NAME ....
ADDRESS ....
....
....